STi

TO THE ROOF

BY TENNESSEE WILLIAMS

PLAYS

Baby Doll & Tiger Tail
Camino Real
Cat on a Hot Tin Roof
Clothes for a Summer Hotel
Dragon Country
The Glass Menagerie
A Lovely Sunday for Creve Coeur
Not About Nightingales
The Notebook of Trigorin
The Red Devil Battery Sign
Small Craft Warnings
Something Cloudy, Something Clear
Spring Storm
Stopped Rocking and Other Screen Plays
A Streetcar Named Desire
Sweet Bird of Youth

THE THEATRE OF TENNESSEE WILLIAMS, VOLUME I
Battle of Angels, A Streetcar Named Desire, The Glass Menagerie
THE THEATRE OF TENNESSEE WILLIAMS, VOLUME II
The Eccentricities of a Nightingale, Summer and Smoke, The Rose Tattoo,
Camino Real
THE THEATRE OF TENNESSEE WILLIAMS, VOLUME III
Cat on a Hot Tin Roof, Orpheus Descending, Suddenly Last Summer
THE THEATRE OF TENNESSEE WILLIAMS, VOLUME IV
Sweet Bird of Youth, Period of Adjustment, The Night of the Iguana
THE THEATRE OF TENNESSEE WILLIAMS, VOLUME V
The Milk Train Doesn't Stop Here Anymore, Kingdom of Earth (The Seven Descents
of Myrtle), Small Craft Warnings, The Two-Character Play
THE THEATRE OF TENNESSEE WILLIAMS, VOLUME VI
27 Wagons Full of Cotton and Other Short Plays
THE THEATRE OF TENNESSEE WILLIAMS, VOLUME VII
In the Bar of a Tokyo Hotel and Other Plays
THE THEATRE OF TENNESSEE WILLIAMS, VOLUME VIII
Vieux Carré, A Lovely Sunday for Creve Coeur, Clothes for a Summer Hotel,
The Red Devil Battery Sign
27 Wagons Full of Cotton and Other Plays
The Two-Character Play
Vieux Carré

POETRY

Androgyne, Mon Amour
In the Winter of Cities

PROSE

Collected Stories
Hard Candy and Other Stories
One Arm and Other Stories
The Roman Spring of Mrs. Stone
Where I Live: Selected Essays

Cover of Playbill for the 1947 Pasadena Playhouse production of
Stairs to the Roof; used courtesy of the Harry Ransom Humanities
Research Center, University of Texas at Austin.

TENNESSEE WILLIAMS

STAIRS TO THE ROOF

A PRAYER FOR THE WILD OF HEART
THAT ARE KEPT IN CAGES

EDITED, WITH AN INTRODUCTION, BY

ALLEAN HALE

A NEW DIRECTIONS BOOK

Thanks are due to the Special Collections of the University of California at Los Angeles Library where the original typescript is housed. Thanks also to the Harry Ransom Humanities Research Center, Austin, Texas, for script variants and especially to Erin Wardlow of the Rare Book Department, The Huntington Library, San Marino, California, for a print of the cover photograph, and to Kristie French, Special Collections, California State University, Long Beach, California, for supplying copies of programs and reviews of the two Pasadena productions of *Stairs to the Roof.*

Special thanks are due to Thomas Keith for his invaluable help in preparing the manuscript. For their help with information, Allean Hale is grateful to Albert J. Devlin and Nancy M. Tischler, editors of *The Selected Letters of Tennessee Williams*, and Margaret Thornton, who is editing Williams' journals. The Editor and Publisher would also like to thank Richard Freeman Leavitt who provided a print of the frontispiece.

Manufactured in the United States of America
New Directions Books are printed on acid-free paper.
First published as New Directions Paperbook 892 in 2000
Published simultaneously in Canada by Penguin Books Canada Limited
Book design by Sylvia Frezzolini Severance

Library of Congress Cataloging-in-Publication Data

Williams Tennessee, 1911-1983.
  Stairs to the roof / Tennessee Williams ; edited with an introduction by Allean Hale.
    p. cm.
  ISBN 0-8112-1435-4 (alk. paper)
1. White collar workers--Drama. I. Hale, Allean, 1914- II. Title.
PS3545.I5365 S73 2000
812'.54—dc21
               99-087704

New Directions books are published for James Laughlin
by New Directions Publishing Corporation,
80 Eighth Avenue, New York 10011

TABLE OF CONTENTS

INTRODUCTION:
A PLAY FOR TOMORROW

Stairs to the Roof is a rare and different Tennessee Williams play; a boy-girl romance with an optimistic ending. The last of his youthful plays, it was his first piece deliberately crafted for Broadway. Having a New York agent, Audrey Wood, made the difference. It was Wood who encouraged him to apply for a Rockefeller Fellowship. The grant of a thousand dollars received in December, 1939, enabled him to escape St. Louis to study under John Gassner at the New School for Social Research in New York. Overnight he was transformed from a jobless "deadbeat," as his unsympathetic father characterized him, to a young man with a future.

In response to war in Europe, the New School was welcoming eminent refugees like Erwin Piscator to its faculty. Piscator's Dramatic Workshop opened January, 1940, with Williams in the first class. The Workshop was designed to put in practice Piscator's avant-garde theatrical techniques: such devices as treadmills, various playing levels, film projections and the documentary approach to narrative which Williams had already used in *Not About Nightingales* (written in 1938). In New York, through his agent, he met Lawrence Langner, founder of the Theatre Guild; Elia Kazan and Eddie Dowling,who would figure in his future; saw the current plays; attended professional rehearsals and so sharpened the tools of his craft. The Playwrights' Seminar chaired by John Gassner and Theresa Helburn, was limited to ten, admission granted on approval of a script, and Williams had brought to New York a long play, *Battle of Angels*, the product of his vagabond trip to Mexico the year before. But evidently he also brought a second script, for he first mentioned *Stairs to the Roof* in his journal of February 12, 1940, as "a rather promising idea about white collar workers." Both Piscator and Gassner recognized Williams' work as exceptional; in February Piscator produced his one-act play, *The Long Goodbye,* in the Studio Theatre—it was Williams' first New York production. Gassner called *Battle of Angels* "the best play done in his class" and showed it to Harold Clurman and Elmer Rice. By May the Theatre Guild had optioned the play, and Tennessee left school for the summer to revise it. However, he seemed more interested in *Stairs to the Roof*, writing Langner: "If someone else were writing it, it might turn out to be a great American drama—there is so much amplitude in the theme." Referring to having attended rehearsals of Odets' *Night Music* he added that he would never release a play—however profound in subject—"till I felt it had sufficient theatricality to make it commercial. Any play that is not 'commercial'—that is, 'good theatre'—is necessarily still-born, isn't it?" By October, he wrote Theresa Helburn that his first long comedy was practically finished, and even in November, with *Battle of Angels* going into rehearsal, Williams told a reporter: "The [play] I'd like most to get on is my 'Stairs to the Roof,' which is a social comedy about a lowly paid clerk trying to escape his economic cage. My interest in social problems is as great as my interest in the theater. . . . " He had already changed his name from Thomas Lanier Williams to "Tennessee."

His concentration on Stairs rather than *Battle of Angels* may have been a form of avoidance. By December, 1940, summoned back to New York to embattled *Battle* rehearsals, the inexperienced author was caught in the maelstrom of casting, rewrite, and production and completely overwhelmed. With Gassner, Williams, Helburn and Langner all frantically working on *Battle,* Williams unwisely accepted changes and corrections from every side, especially from Helburn, executive director of the Guild. *Battle of Angels* opened in Boston on December 30 and quickly closed, censored for mixing sex with religion. The chastened play-wright went off to Key West to rewrite *Battle* and to perfect *Stairs to the Roof*.

The evolution of *Stairs* as a play shows the complex way in which Williams developed a script. At least four early stories fed into the play. "A System of Wheels" describes the daily life of an office worker who is depressed by his routine job but continues on his treadmill. "The Swan" is an extended treatment of Ben's love episode with the Girl. A sketch called "Beauty and the Beast" became the play-within-the-play of the Carnival scene. *Stairs* evolved most directly from a story of the same title written in October, 1936, the fall after Williams' recovery from the nervous breakdown which freed him from his job in the shoe factory (see Editor's Note, p. xxii) Here the clerk is Edward Schiller, a young poet, just as Williams thought of himself at the time. The story opens with a body splattering on the pavement. In a series of flashbacks it excerpts the life of Schiller who, discovered writing poems on company time, is fired in front of the entire office, grows hysterical and jumps from the roof to his death.

The story is especially interesting for Williams' description of the job which caused his own breakdown—apparently the only such account in any of his writing."You insert a sheet of paper (form No. 246-M) in your Ditto machine. . . . At the top of the page . . . you type the name of that particular one of the company's forty-odd factories ...then you type the number of the order, the date, the number of cases, and the number of dozens it contains. . . . Across and down the sheet you go for page after page after page, typing stock numbers. . . . " Schiller's mental state as he types numbers eight hours a day is described: "The duplicating machine is a monster with gaping jaws that will . . . crush him between its gelatined rolls, if he doesn't feed it fast enough . . . the ticking clock that might have brought deliverance is now an axe hanging over his head...the pile of untyped orders climbs higher . . . the penciled digits he is copying have a maddening way of creeping close to his eyes until they appear enormous. . . . His temples are throbbing . . . his haunches are sore. . . . " This description was transposed into stage action as the mechanized opening scene of *Stairs to the Roof*, and the story formed the background of Benjamin Murphy, the play's protagonist.

Converting tragedy to comedy sacrificed some of the poetry for a crisp, energetic dialogue entirely new in Tennessee Williams' work, but he retained the serious subtitle, "A Prayer for the Wild of Heart That are Kept in Cages." Ben works in a shirt factory and has a nagging wife. In trouble for his frequent trips to the washroom, where he writes poetry, he discovers unused stairs to the factory roof where he can escape to view wider horizons. This is the reality of his everyday life until he meets the Girl, a secretary also trapped in a dead-end job, and the two escape on a series of romantic adventures. Back at the factory, their mutual support enables each to rebel. The Girl, who has discovered she loves Ben, not her boss, confronts her employer with his treatment of her as a nonentity and throws away his clock. Ben, about to be fired when his boss and stockholders discover his mysterious stairs, leads a general insurrection of the office workers to the roof. Conveniently, Ben's wife has left him, freeing him for a happy—and even more fantastic—final adventure with the Girl.

Stairs to the Roof is set in the St. Louis of 1933–36, as is *The Glass Menagerie*, which takes place in a drab apartment. The interior scenes in *Stairs* are equally drab, but the fantasy scenes are set outdoors in the city's Forest Park, with its lagoon, and on its outskirts, the Highlands, a large amusement complex. In the park was the Municipal Opera, the country's largest outdoor theatre. Here Williams saw his first professional productions, and their choruses, dancers, and sets introduced him to theatre as spectacle. Remembering the "Muny" may have influenced him to write into *Stairs* a cast of thirty-one, a chorus, and a spectacular ending.

Besides being his first long comedy, *Stairs* was the last of his apprentice plays. The others, *Candles to the Sun*, *Fugitive Kind*, *Not About Nightingales*, *Spring Storm* and the concurrent *Battle of Angels* were all essentially tragic. *Stairs* would be affirmative—

and Tennessee vowed, a commercial success. He made a list of the plays he admired, especially those of prizewinning playwrights, but his first influence was an actor. "I have written the part of Benjamin Murphy with Burgess Meredith in mind," Williams wrote in his foreword and gave his spunky little hero the initials, B.M. Williams would write with a specific actor in mind throughout his career, usually choosing a top star. He had seen Meredith in Maxwell Anderson's *Winterset* in St. Louis on stage and in film and had written in his journal: "Burgess Meredith is an exquisitely fine actor." Anderson's *High Tor*, in which a man and girl thwart commercial developers may have also influenced him.

But the specific play which comes to mind as a model for *Stairs to the Roof* is *The Adding Machine* by Elmer Rice. Both plays show the workers typing like robots, have a scene by a lake, and an instance of divine intervention. Williams uses his Messrs. P, D, Q, T, to represent the impersonality of the workplace. Rice has Messrs. One, Two, Three, Four, etc. voice the prejudices of society. He calls his male lead "Mr. Zero"; Williams calls his female lead "Girl." If he did borrow ideas from the established playwright, it was perhaps a deliberate tribute to Rice and another move in his campaign to get his play staged. Like all writers, Williams got ideas from his predecessors; the new ways he built on them made them unique. Finally it was his contemporary, William Saroyan, with whom he would often be compared. Almost the same age, both were rebels against a society which they sought to change. Fresh young voices in the theatre, each brought a new freedom and impressionistic concept of playwriting to the stage. The two were inevitable competitors as each produced a new one-act or full length play each year. Saroyan won the Pulitzer Prize in 1940, Williams won it in 1947; his star rose as Saroyan's descended. Some critics would call *Stairs* "Saroyanish", but where Saroyan was fey to the extreme, Williams was more disciplined.

The script of *Stairs to the Roof* demonstrates his new sophistication. Where *Not About Nightingales* was sometimes careless in accounting for situations and characters, and where *Battle of Angels* tried to crowd all of his concerns into one play, *Stairs* is a model of craftsmanship. The opening set is dominated by a huge clock, the controlling metaphor of the play, suggesting the mechanical, relentless world where individuals are ruled by a machine. The opening lines introduce the plot—where is Ben? The Designer's entrance sets a comedic tone and provides exposition—this is a shirt factory; the initial scene between Mr. Gum and Ben establishes dramatic conflict and lets Ben introduce the play's theme: "people have got to find stairs to the roof." As the scene ends in a stalemate between his boss and Ben, the plot poses three questions: Will Ben be fired? Where are the stairs to the roof? Whose is the mysterious offstage laugh which comments on the action? All of this is accomplished in the first few pages of script. The Clock in some form is a reminder in almost every scene, and each scene skillfully advances the plot by developing suspense. Conflict is furthered by characters who bring the idealistic Ben down to earth, his wife Alma, Mr. Gum, his college friend Jim. Ben is poetic, philosophical, dreamy; Jim is pragmatic, sardonic, realistic. When Boy meets Girl romance enters the plot but when this results in a sexual embrace, the tone is ironic rather than sentimental, as each mentally substitutes another for the real person in the action. With their romance the play shifts from realism towards fantasy, culminating in the Carnival scene and "Beauty and the Beast," the Mummers' show. This was conceived as "the orgasmic center of the play, representing the . . . dreams of childhood." This seems more relevant if we recall the Jean Cocteau film of *Beauty and the Beast* which Williams, the movie-goer, probably saw, with its surreal ending of the lovers floating into space. The action when Ben jumps to the stage and delivers his speech on brotherhood seems a direct precursor of *Camino Real* as does the chase where he knocks down the guard and frees the foxes in the zoo. When Ben tells the Girl he is married, the play moves back to reality, with a series of short scenes showing Ben and Jim each trapped in a miserable marriage. The ending returns to the play's beginning as board members and boss confront the mutiny and are forced to follow their workers to the roof. There Ben and the Girl finally meet Mr. E who effects their fantastic escape as the entire cast celebrates. Williams asked his agent if this ending was too frankly a *deus ex machina.* Fortunately, rather than go for a more conventional solution, the young playwright's instinct was to let it stand.

In his play synopsis Williams stated, "Written for stage or screen," which may be why there are few stage directions, as if he were leaving these to a future director. Minimal furniture and no props called for some action to be pantomimed. His few descriptions are expressionistic: "the eerie blue atmosphere of a landscape by . . . Dali," a clue to the surreal nature of the play; skyscraper towers pointing upward "like so many fingers." "Projected on the backdrop," he writes. This seems to be the first example of Williams using film projections. The stairs are not shown, although when the play was finally produced their image dominated the set: a spiral curving upward and out of sight. They may represent the play's ascending movement from reality to fantasy, as Nancy Tischler suggests; they also symbolize the upward movement towards a new life. In his script requirements, the playwright broke any bounds of commercialism and freed the true Williams, for whom anything imagined was possible. From the large cast to the final airborne escape, he challenged the practicalities of production. His aim was to use every medium possible to the stage. Music was indicated throughout, to set the mood or comment on the action. Expressionism combines with realism in his characters as it does in the play. Although Ben represents the universal "little man," Williams' projection of Burgess Meredith as Murphy tied him to realism. Also, Ben is the Tennessee Williams figure and Jim was a real character, Jim Connor, a college friend. Jim's wife with her "Rise and shine." is a less flattering portrait of Williams' mother. The characters based on real people were seen realistically; the generalized characters were more expressionistic.

For today's audience, *Stairs to the Roof* has certain gender issues which should be considered in the light of yesterday's mores. To portray a gay character in 1941 was still daring. In the original script the Designer was called "An Effeminate Man" and presented the comedic portrait of a gay male then acceptable on the commercial stage. (This was the era of *Charley's Aunt*, the tremendously popular transvestite farce.) This stereotype may have been Williams' ultimate nod to commercialism, for in *Not About Nightingales*, he had portrayed a homosexual sympathetically. In the 1945 Pasadena production "Effeminate Man" was changed to "The Designer." In the politically correct atmosphere of the year 2000, the issue might be avoided by casting the designer as a woman. Williams does interpolate lines in the final scene which may be his defense of homosexuality, when Mr. E refers to the "sorry mess that having two sexes has made of things." Another problem for today's critics is The Girl. The label suggests a generic female. Ben pictures her in turn as sexual object, Madonna, and mother figure—all masculine cliches. The Girl's own assertions that "love is a woman's Wonderland" give us pause today. The fact that the Girl is in love with her boss cancels our potential sympathy for her as a victim, although he does victimize her by not even remembering her name. She is delightful as a character, but we want her to develop rather than travel through the play as an appendage to Ben. It is when she confronts her boss that she becomes real. If Williams was using his sister as model, he may not have wanted to get too close to reality, preferring to recall the fairy-tale days of their childhood. There is one reference to Rose in the play, when Bertha warns her roommate of having known a girl with *dementia praecox*— Rose's diagnosis.

Knowing that this play was written as the United States went into World War II, one may ask why war has no more presence in the drama. It is actually referred to in almost every scene but is submerged by the playwright's comedic intent. Later Williams wrote that war should only be described by soldiers. As his foreword says, "Wars come and wars go . . . but Benjamin Murphy

and [his] problems . . . go on forever." The growing impersonality
of American life, the dehumanization of man in an increasingly
mechanistic world, those nameless individuals whose humdrum
existence prevents any fulfillment—these are the concerns of *Stairs
to the Roof*. In its way, the play is very American, patriotic in its
plea for individual liberty and the pursuit of happiness. Williams
wrote in his *Note to Potential Producers:* "I wish that I were sufficiently an economic or political theorist to advance a scheme for
correction of these unlucky circumstances which I have tried to
show. As it is, I can only show them. . . ." After Pearl Harbor,
which he wrote was "the end of the world as we know it," he finished his script and by Christmas wrote that the play "shines very
brightly in places. It is all I really have to say. Said about as well as
I am able to say it right now." He signed it "T. Wms., New
Orleans, Dec. 1941." And to Audrey Wood he wrote, "this may
be more a play for tomorrow than today. . . . Today is pretty
dreadful, isn't it?" Audrey sent him a copy of his draft card that
she held in safe-keeping—4-F because of his poor eyesight.

He had had a hopeful episode in November when Piscator
proposed to revive *Battle of Angels* as a studio production.
Desperate as Williams was for money, when he realized that
Piscator had rewritten his play as an anti-Faschist polemic, he
withdrew it. Hume Cronyn had taken an ongoing option on his
short plays, and with the $25 a month installments his only
dependable source of income, Williams was steadily turning out
one-acts. He was also working on a trilogy, *The Americans,*
which he had proposed to Audrey as early as 1939. *Daughter of
Revolution* would be a sort of "Life With Mother" portrait; *The
Aristocrats* would portray an artistic woman forced into prosti-
tution by poverty. Now he thought of using *Stairs to the Roof*, his
own story, as the third play. Audrey had sent *Stairs* to producer
David Merrick and in June, 1942, Tennessee received the answer
which seemed to seal that play's fate. Merrick had found the
script "interesting and beautifully written" but opined, "I don't
think a producer would be likely to risk a more than average

amount of production money on a fantasy . . . at this time. Not unless it had a chorus of pretty girls, and a part for Gertrude Lawrence."

When *Stairs* was finally performed on March 25, 1945, at the little Pasadena Playbox the timing was out of joint. *The Glass Menagerie* had just finished its triumphal Chicago run and was moving to Broadway, to win all "Best Play of the Year" awards. By 1944 the playwright was making $1000 a week and his treatise on the penniless clerk seemed nostalgic rather than propagandistic. When *Stairs* had a mainstage production at the Pasadena Playhouse on February 26, 1947, *A Streetcar Named Desire* was about to hit Broadway like a bomb. The optimistic *Stairs* would no longer represent the Tennessee Williams who wrote tragedy and was being hailed as the new Eugene O'Neill.

Williams did not go to see *Stairs*, although the Playhouse, one of the two best regional theatres in the United States, gave his play a lavish production. Seven of the dozen reviews were enthusiastic, calling it impassioned, provocative, poetic, a play "in the modern manner" but not "arty." Apparently Williams read only the first, from *Daily Variety*, which, he wrote Audrey, "was no accolade." "Stairs to the Roof Rickety," called the play "Williams' crackpot, alleged theatrical piece." Since the reviewer did not identify himself and also disparaged *The Glass Menagerie*, his opinion can be dismissed.

Although Williams would never again write a play as light-hearted as *Stairs to the Roof*, he never relinquished his love of fantasy. This strain of fantasy fed into *Camino Real*, which his agent advised him to hide immediately. Not till after the Royal Shakespeare production of 1988 did *Camino* win universal praise. Was *Stairs to the Roof* indeed "a play for tomorrow," as its author speculated fifty-eight years ago? Its science-fiction ending, predating the inter-galactic explorations of *2001: A Space Odyssey* and *Star Trek* is on target today. Ben's quarrel with the clock—man against machine—was contemporized as the year 2000 approached when a computer-programming oversight had far-reaching economic effects. Today's machine is the computer, and Ben's contemporary concern might be whether mankind will become its victim. Meanwhile, there are still little people toiling at dehumanizing jobs and dreaming of freedom. In his autobiography, *Timebends*, Arthur Miller wrote that Tennessee Williams wanted to change the world. *Stairs to the Roof* still testifies as a plea for that change.

ALLEAN HALE

RANDOM OBSERVATIONS

This play is written for both the stage and the screen and the part of Benjamin D. Murphy was created with Burgess Meredith in mind. It was written involuntarily as a katharsis of eighteen months that I once spent as a clerk in a large wholesale corporation in the Middle West. This eighteen months' interlude, my season in hell, came at a time when I was just out of high school and the world appeared to be a place of infinite and exciting possibilities. I discovered how badly mistaken it is possible for a young man to be.

I escaped to college.

I left the others behind me—Eddie, Doretta, Nora, Jimmie, Dell—and I never went back to see if they were still there. I believe they are.

THIS PLAY IS DEDICATED TO THEM.

I dedicate it to them and to all of the other little wage-earners of the world not only with affection, but with profound respect and earnest prayer.

I know that there is a good deal of didactic material in this play, some of which will probably burden the reader. When I was half way through it the United States of America went to war. For a moment I wondered if I should continue the work. Or should I immediately undertake the composition of something light and frothy not only in spirit but matter? I decided not to. I am not so good at writing what I want to write that I can afford to write something else. So I kept on . . . with this feeling about it. Wars come and wars go and this one will be no exception. But Benjamin Murphy and Benjamin Murphy's problems are universal and everlasting. Also—this! Volcanic eruptions are not the result of disturbances in the upper part of the crater; something way, way down—basic and fundamental—is at the seat of the trouble. At the bottom of our social architecture, which is now describing such perilous gyrations in mid-air, are the unimportant little Benjamin Murphys and their problems . . . and if there is something at the bottom that started the trouble on top, what could be more appropriate at this moment than inspecting the bottom?

Let's take a look!

T. WMS.
NEW ORLEANS
DEC. 1941

EDITOR'S NOTE

In his "random observations" Williams has obviously adjusted the chronology of events to fit his recently adjusted birthdate. He was not "just out of high school" when he went to the shoe factory, but at age 22 just out of his third year at the University of Missouri. Likewise, his "escape" was to Washington University in 1936 at age 25. At the end of 1938, while he was at home jobless, penniless, and desperate, he learned of a Group Theatre playwriting contest for writers under 25. Tom was 27, but felt justified in dropping the years spent at the factory as "lost time." He sent four one-acts under the title *American Blues*, and two long plays, *Fugitive Kind* and *Not About Nightingales*, for the first time signing himself "Tennessee Williams." Winning an award of one hundred dollars for his one-act plays brought him to the attention of agent Audrey Wood who launched his Broadway career.

Williams never had a deep regard for reality, but his lie caught up with him through the years. *Stairs to the Roof*, with its obviously autobiographical college graduation scene was perhaps the first example. As biographers listed his birthdate as 1914 instead of 1911 and reporters delved into his background, the dissimulation about his age grew troublesome. It was when Kenneth Tynan in 1955 proposed to write a major piece on the playwright that Williams finally confronted the myth, writing Tynan: "I think it would be fitting for you to give the true date of my birth, March 26, 1911."

A. H.

PRODUCTION NOTES

Stairs to the Roof was first performed in 1945 in a laboratory setting, The Pasadena Playbox, an intimate space used for experimental productions. Seating only 50 persons, subscribers and invited guests, it was closed to the general public and to reporters. Gilmor Brown was the Director, assisted by Beatrice Hassell.

On February 26, 1947, the play opened at the Pasadena Playhouse, for a full-scale production directed by Gilmor Brown and Rita Glover, assisted by Julia Farnsworth. An elaborate musical background was arranged by Jack Curtiss; Fred C. Huxley was Technical Director.

Stairs to the Roof will have a twenty-first century premiere at the Krannert Center for the Performing Arts at the University of Illinois-Urbana from November 2 through 12, 2000. Staged in the Studio Theatre, a newly equipped space seating 250, it will feature the latest in computer-assisted scenery. Thomas Mitchell is the Director; Lee Boyer is the Production Design Supervisor. A Symposium of Tennessee Williams scholars and theatre practitioners is planned in conjunction with the play.

CHARACTERS

The cast of characters, in order of appearance, is as follows:

MR. GUM
ALFRED
JOHNNIE, *The Office Boy*
A DESIGNER
BENJAMIN D. MURPHY
MR. WARREN B. THATCHER
THE GIRL
JIM
THE BARTENDER
BERTHA
ALMA, *Ben's Wife*
HELEN
A YOUNG SOLDIER
EDNA, *Jim's Wife*
THE POLICEMAN
A VAGRANT
THE NIGHT WATCHMAN (*also* THE ZOO KEEPER)
TWO ZOO GUARDS
THE CLOWN
FIRST MUMMER (READER)
BEAUTY
THE BEAST
MRS. HOTCHKISS
ALMA'S MOTHER
MESSRS. P, D, Q, T, *Company Stockholders*
MR. E (*Whose great laughter is heard frequently during the play but who makes no appearance until the final scene.*)

OFFICE WORKERS, CHORAL VOICES, OFFSTAGE SPEAKERS,
CARNIVAL CROWD, A BARKER

Stairs to the Roof

Jack be nimble,
Jack be quick
Jack jump over
Arithmetic!

SCENE ONE

"SHIRTS AND THE UNIVERSE"

The curtain rises on a department of Continental Shirtmakers. There is only the minimum equipment on the stage, such as Mr. Gum's desk and the enormous clock at the front of the office. The rest is suggested by the movements of the workers. They sit on stools, their arms and hands making rigid, machine-like motions above their imaginary desks to indicate typing, filing, operating a comptometer, and so forth. Two middle-aged women are reciting numbers to each other, antiphonally, in high and sing-song voices. The girl at the (invisible) filing cabinet has the far-away stare of a schizophrenic as her arms work mechanically above the indexed cases. There is a glassy brilliance to the atmosphere: one feels that it must contain a highly selected death ray that penetrates living tissue straight to the heart and bestows a withering kiss on whatever diverges from an accepted pattern.

Gum is glancing at an enormous sales record book; he suddenly slams it down on the desk.

GUM [*bellowing*]: Alfred!

ALFRED [*turning quickly, snake-like*]: Yes, sir?

GUM: Where's Murphy?

ALFRED: He's been away from his desk about six minutes!

GUM [*to the office boy*]: Johnnie, go fetch Murphy out of the washroom.

JOHNNIE: He's not in the washhroom, Mr. Gum.

GUM: How do you know?

JOHNNIE: I just been.

GUM: Fetch him out of the warehouse, then.

ALFRED: He's not in the warehouse either, Mr. Gum. —*I* just been.

GUM: Well, where the hell is he then?

ALFRED: I don't know, Mr. Gum. He disappears like this every once in a while.

GUM: Where does he disappear to?

ALFRED: That is a mystery, Mr. Gum.

GUM: We don't have any mysteries in the Continental Branch of Consolidated Shirtmakers.

ALFRED: I didn't think we did. But Benjamin Murphy seems to have created one for us.

GUM: Aw, created one, has he? Johnnie, go look for Murphy and bring him back dead or alive.

[*An effeminate young man enters rapidly from the rear holding a stiff-front colored shirt.*]

DESIGNER: Oh, Mr. Gum, this No. W-2-O wasn't made up according to specifications! The stripes on the dickey should have been pale, *pale* blue but they're *al*-most *pur*-ple!

[*Gum glares at him ominously.*]

These little accessory buttons are mother-of-pearl— [*He rolls his eyes heavenward.*] —I don't know what type of person would wear a shirt like this!

GUM: You don't but I do! —Take it up with Frankel in Specifications.

[*The Designer exits quickly one hand to forehead, the other holding the dickey thrust out behind him. Ben Murphy enters. He is a small young man with the nervous, defensive agility of a squirrel. Ten years of regimentation have made him frantic but have not subdued his spirit. He is one of those feverish, bright little people who might give God some very intelligent answers if they were asked. He has on white duck pants, a shirt with broad blue and white stripes, and—oddly enough—a pair of cowboy boots.*]

GUM [*with a bull-like roar*]: MURPHY!

[*Ben halts, paralyzed for a moment. He turns slowly to face the boss. His eyebrows climb in tense, polite enquiry.*]

Murphy, come here to my desk.

[*Ben crosses stiffly to Gum. Gum looking him up and down.*]

What's the idea of coming down to work in an outfit like that? That belt—emerald studded?

BEN: A souvenir of a summer in Arizona a long time ago. I wear the belt to be reminded of it.

GUM: No matter how small a man's position may be, it still has got some dignity attached to it.

BEN: Yes, sir.

GUM: Where have you been for the last ten—fifteen minutes?

BEN: Been? I—went to the washroom.

GUM: Johnnie's just been in the washroom and says you weren't there.

BEN: I also went to the warehouse for a minute.

GUM: Alfred's just come from the warehouse. He didn't see you.

BEN: Well—I—I went upstairs for a minute.

GUM: You went upstairs. Murphy, you may not know it, but you have just now made a remarkable statement.

BEN: How is that, Mr. Gum?

GUM: You say you went upstairs. To my best knowledge, Continental Branch of Consolidated Shirtmakers is on the sixteenth floor of a sixteen-story building.

BEN: I know that, Mr. Gum.

GUM: Then—how did you—go *upstairs*?

BEN: Mr. Gum, you probably never dreamed of such a thing but—there's a stairs to the roof.

GUM: A *what*?

BEN: A stairs to the roof.

[*Activity in the office is momentarily suspended. Everyone stares at Ben.*]

GUM: So there is a stairs to the roof?

BEN: Yes, sir.

GUM: How did you find out about it, Murphy?

BEN: Necessity, Mr. Gum. I was stifling in here.

GUM [*ominously*]: I see. Necessity being the mother of invention, you finally came to invent the stairs to the roof.

BEN: No, sir, I didn't invent them, they were already there, just waiting to be discovered.

GUM: And you discovered them?

BEN: Yes, sir.

GUM: I suppose you might be termed the Christopher Columbus of the Consolidated roof—and who was, so to speak, your Queen Isabella?

BEN: Curiosity, Mr. Gum. One day I noticed a little door at the top of the elevator shaft. I simply opened it and there they were— a little, narrow, winding flight of stairs that led to the roof.

GUM: Well!

BEN: After that, instead of smoking my cigarette in the wash- room with the rest of the boys, I smoked it up there where I could take a look at the world, the sky, the bluffs across the river—and I must say it's definitely more inspiring to look at them than the plumbing fixtures in the men's lavatory. Also the air up there's a whole lot cleaner and fresher.

[*Pause.*]

GUM: The air down here don't suit you?

BEN: No, sir. I can't say it does. Since they've had that new cooling system installed we're not allowed to open up the windows. — Frankly the air in here gets just as thick as molasses. The air outside is hot—but even so you don't know what a blessed relief it can be to step out there and fill your lungs with it and know it's exclusively yours and not just borrowed a moment from somebody at the next desk.

GUM: Aw. —Uh-huh. Well, Murphy, I guess we'll have to scrap that fifty-thousand dollar cooling system now that it don't agree with your—respiratory system!

BEN: I didn't say to scrap it, Mr. Gum. But just to—revise it a little.

GUM [*getting warmed up*]: Or build you a little private office, a penthouse kind of, where you can associate with pigeons.

BEN: Pigeons are very good company, Mr. Gum.

GUM: Especially for you, Mr. Murphy.

BEN: Sure. We have lots in common.

GUM: And just about the same amount of intelligence, too.

BEN: No, sir, pigeons are smarter than me—a whole lot.

GUM: You admit it?

BEN: Yes, sir. They take the liberty of the sky. Me, Mr. Gum, I never get any further than the roof.

GUM [*rising abruptly*]: Your work in this office has placed too many restrictions on your freedom.

BEN: Freedom, Mr. Gum, is something my forefathers had when they marched down through Cumberland Gap with horses and women and guns to make a new world. They made it and lost it. Sold it down the river for cotton and slaves and various other commodities sold at a profit created by cheating each other.

GUM [*furious and alarmed*]: Be careful, Murphy!

BEN: There hasn't been very much freedom in the world since. There's still the need of it, though. So people have got to find stairs to the roof.

GUM: *Hush up*! This isn't the fourth of July!

BEN: I'm not shooting off firecrackers.

GUM: You're not, but I am! [*He shoves the sales record book in front of Ben.*] What's this?

BEN: It looks like the August sales record book to me.

GUM: That's what I thought it was. What's this here got to do with "white broadcloth, tab collar, reinforced cuff seam, style number X92"?

BEN [*pointing*]: This?

GUM: Yes, that. Read it out loud, Murphy, so everyone here in the office can get a load of it.

BEN: I can't.

GUM: Why not?

BEN: It's private.

GUM: *Read* it, Murphy.

BEN: *The earth is a—wheel—*

GUM: I said to read it out *loud*, Murphy.

BEN [*shouting*]: *The earth is a wheel—in a great big gambling casino!*

[*The office workers stop short in their mechanical activity. Alfred's giggle gives them the cue and they titter for several moments.*]

GUM: Did you intend for that statement to be embroidered on the back of your shirts?

BEN: No, sir.

GUM: Then why did you put it in our business records? Did it appear to you to have some particular bearing on broadcloth shirts?

BEN: No particular bearing.

GUM: Aw. But a general bearing?

BEN: It seems to me, Mr. Gum, that reflections on the nature of the universe have got some general bearing on everything there is.

GUM: We have a philosopher here—Benjamin Murphy, Ph. D.

BEN: No, sir, only B.A.

GUM: B.A. your—! Is this a kindergarten for your amusement?

BEN: I didn't write that for amusement.

GUM: What for, then?

BEN: Because it's—instinct with an artist—to find some means of expression.

GUM: A what? An artist? —So you're an artist, are you?

BEN [*wildly*]: I didn't say that! You're putting words in my mouth!

[*Alfred giggles.*]

[*Ben continues, turning desperately.*] Make that ape stop giggling! [*He seizes Alfred by the collar.*] Stop that giggling, you ape! [*Ben chokes him, forcing Alfred down to his knees.*]

ALFRED: Help, help, help, Mr. Gum!

GUM: Murphy!

[*The Designer bustles in. He shrieks at the scene of violence. The bell in the clock rings for noon with a piercing clamor.*]

Murphy, let Alfred go!

[*Murphy reluctantly lets go of the spindling stool pigeon.*]

This is the first time in my twenty-five years as a—manager of this department that anyone's made such a scene! [*To the office*]: You all go to lunch! —Murphy, you stay here.

[*The workers file rapidly out with timid, backward glances. Murphy is left alone with the boss. Murphy's bravado deserts him. Now he is white and trembling. He suddenly collapses into a chair and covers his face. Gum continues, lighting a cigar.*]

Apparently you are beginning to realize the enormity of your actions.

BEN [*brokenly*]: Yes, sir. [*He blows his nose.*]

GUM: Why don't you comb your hair, Murphy?

BEN: I do but it won't stay down.

GUM: Even your hair—rebellious! I remember the morning you first came here to look for a job. A fresh young college boy, clean looking, alert, ambitious. Maybe a little too smart in your use of the language, but I figured that would wear off in time. I said to myself, "Here is a possibility for Continental Branch of Consolidated Shirtmakers. Give this boy an office job so he can get the necessary background—then put him on the road where he can put to use these more individual characteristics of his."

BEN: Mr. Gum—

GUM: Two years—three years—six years. No development. Oh, you did your work, you got down here at the usual time every morning—but what you gave was just a routine performance, nothing to single you out as a man who deserved to be given his chance on the road.

BEN: Mr. Gum—

GUM: Yes?

BEN: Let me ask you a question, just as one member of the race of man to another— What chance does anyone have to develop "individual characteristics" in a place like this? I'm not a great social thinker, I'm not very much of a political theorist, Mr. Gum. But there's a disease in the world, a terrible fever, and sooner or later it's got to be rooted out or the patient will die. People wouldn't be killing and trying to conquer each other unless there was something terribly, terribly wrong at the bottom of things. It just occurs to me, Mr. Gum, that maybe the wrong is this: this regimentation, this gradual grinding out of the lives of the little people under the thumbs of things that are bigger than they are! People get panicky locked up in a dark cellar: they trample over each other fighting for air! Air, air, give them air! Isn't it maybe— just as simple as that?

[*The bell at the front of the office sets up another harsh clamor. The workers return from their lunch. Gum stares dumbly at Murphy and Murphy stares dumbly at Gum.*]

GUM [*finally*]: You have a wife?

BEN: Yes, sir.

GUM: Children?

BEN: Not yet. One's expected.

GUM: I intend to look back through your records from "a" to "z." If I can discover any ray of hope for your future with Continental Branch of the Consolidated Shirtmakers, I'll let you stay on here. But if I don't find any— Then out you'll go, Ben Murphy, regardless of the wife or the stork or any other tender consideration. —You understand that?

BEN: Yes, sir.

13

GUM: Come back to my desk at exactly noon tomorrow and I'll let you know.

BEN [*faintly*]: Yes, sir.

GUM: Go on! Get back to your work!

BEN: Yes, sir. [*He turns mechanically and marches back to his desk. He slowly raises an enormous ledger to cover his agonized face.*]

[*Everyone works with puppet-like precision. The middle-aged spinsters recite their numerals in high and sing-song voices. Gum sits glowering for a moment in his swivel chair at the great yellow oak desk. Then suddenly he wheels the chair about to face the audience. He spreads his arms in a wide and helpless gesture—it is the gesture of Pilate—"What can I do?"*]

FADE

[*Mr. E laughs offstage.*]

"NO FIRE ESCAPE"

The scene is the legal office of Mr. Warren B. Thatcher, several floors down in the same office building. The office is suggested with only essential equipment.

Seated behind a modernistic desk is Mr. Thatcher, a good-looking young man in his middle thirties; he wears a white linen suit, a pale blue tie, and a very grim expression.

As the curtain rises, he speaks into the phone.

THATCHER [*into the phone*]: Hello, my darling. I'm calling to give you some dreadful information. I'm way up high in a building that's caught on fire. There's no way out. There aren't any fire-escapes, there don't seem to be any fire-extinguishers even. —And as for the volunteer fire department, darling—it hasn't volunteered! What am I talking about? —The state of the world we live in! It's cracking up, it's plunging toward destruction! What did we quarrel about last night, you and I? Oh, yes, I remember, I didn't feel like dancing but you did!

[*The Girl comes in, small and shy and harmlessly attractive. She wears a pink linen dress and carries a cup in trembling hands. Her adoration of Mr. Thatcher is instantly apparent.*]

GIRL [*breathlessly*]: Here, Mr. Thatcher.

THATCHER [*covering mouthpiece of the phone*]: What's that?

GIRL: Water.

THATCHER: I don't want water. I want a Coca-Cola.

GIRL: Oh, I'll get you one. [*She hurries out.*]

THATCHER [*into the phone*]: Sent my office-girl out. I've had three in the last three months and all of them fell in love with me. I have a dreadful suspicion that this one is on the verge of declaring her passion. Why don't you? —I know you do. —I've got to see you. —Tell him whatever you please, but meet me tonight. Tonight at the "Care-free Cabins" on Highway 60. I love you.

[*The Girl enters.*]

Back already?

GIRL: They have a vending-machine in the hall, Mr. Thatcher. Did you want me to stay out a little while longer?

THATCHER [*sharply*]: No. [*Into the phone*]: Remember tonight, the "Carefree Cabins," at half-past ten. Good-bye. [*He immediately snatches up a piece of paper.*] I have here a letter from a Mr. Otto K. Deisseldorff of Pascagoula, Mississippi. —Mr. Deisseldorff's letter states that a very mysterious odor has been detectable in his mercantile store ever since our clients installed their stripping. Customers notice this odor as soon as they enter. They enter and sniff and turn around and walk out and Mr. Deisseldorff hasn't the slightest doubt that this is because of the very mysterious odor. He states, moreover, that he is a nervous wreck, he has been to the doctor not once but fifteen times at the cost of two-fifty per visit. The walls, the floor, and every inch of the woodwork has just been thoroughly scrubbed with scalding hot water containing a strong solution of Clorox disinfectant. And still the peculiar mysterious odor continues. Therefore Mr. Deisseldorff states, in this five-page letter of his, he feels not only justified in refusing to make our clients any payment but also believes that he ought to sue our clients for damages amounting to at least ten thousand dollars! [*He drops the paper.*] Now let's take a look at our client's correspondence.

GIRL: Which do you mean?

THATCHER [*sharply*]: The weather-stripping concern! What is the matter? Why do you look so blank?

GIRL: What was the name of the weather-stripping concern?

THATCHER: I can't remember the name of the weather-stripping concern. But surely *you* do!

GIRL: I'm dreadfully sorry—I don't!

THATCHER: It is because you're so acutely concerned about the collapse of modern civilization that you can't think?

GIRL: I really don't know if it's about that or not, but somehow or other I can't seem to concentrate!

THATCHER: What are you doing there now?

GIRL: I'm looking it up in the files.

THATCHER: Under what letter, please?

GIRL [*panicky*]: I don't remember.

THATCHER: If you could remember! A very useful thing, a memory! Yes indeed! What's those things in your hands?

GIRL: Papers!

THATCHER: Papers, yes, paper! I didn't suppose they were sheets of aluminum plate!

[*The Girl nervously drops the papers.*]

What did you do that for?

GIRL: I couldn't help it.

THATCHER: You must have butterfingers. —Oh, my God!

[*They simultaneously bend to pick up the papers and butt their heads together. Both straighten up with agonized expressions. The Girl suddenly covers her face and sobs hysterically.*]

Nerves?

GIRL: Yes—yes!

THATCHER: I'm sorry.

GIRL: I'm sorry about my dress.

THATCHER: Your what? —Your dress? —Why? Is something spilt on it?

GIRL: No. —You don't like pink. You have an allergy to it.

THATCHER: What? Really, this sounds a little bit fantastic!

GIRL: I know it does. But don't you remember? The day I applied for the job I had this pink dress on. You laughed and said, "I'd rather you didn't wear pink! —I have an allergy to it!"

THATCHER: Oh. —Did I say that?

GIRL: Yes, and I *did* remember. I didn't wear it on purpose. But everything else I had was in the wash. Please—please excuse me!

THATCHER: Do sit down and compose yourself, young lady. I'm going to take the rest of the afternoon off. I think I need it. After you've finished pulling yourself together— [*He puts on his*

Panama hat.] I wish you'd try to find that correspondence! [*Hesitantly he touches her shoulder.*] Good afternoon!

GIRL: Good—

[*He closes the door.*]

—bye.

[*She moves slowly, in a daze, to the desk and picks up the Dictaphone and continues softly.*]

Dear Mr. Thatcher. I have lost my mind. Not because of the collapse of modern civilization. But because of *love*, Mr. Thatcher. I'm in love. I'm terribly in love! Oh, Mr. Thatcher, why did you have to be such a *beautiful* person?

BLACKOUT

[*Mr. E laughs offstage.*]

SCENE THREE

"THE SCENE OF CELEBRATION"

A spot lights two tables and a jukebox in a downtown bar. A funeral wreath surrounds a placard which says: In Memory of our Credit Man.

Jim is seated at one of the two round tables—with an enormous twenty-six ounce glass of beer.

Bertha sits at the other.

Jim is a heavy-set fellow of thirty who looks somewhat older. He has a strong face beginning to go slack from tedium and a deep unconscious despair.

Bertha is a girl of twenty-five, who demonstrates vacuum cleaners in a department store. When she goes out on a date she loses her head and talks too much and makes her palpitations too apparent if the man does not call up for a second engagement. She has a lot of girlfriends, who meet once a week for contract bridge and try to excel each other in the preparation of refreshments, so that now what was originally "a little snack" between rubbers has turned into something like a Roman banquet. The girls are all getting heavy.

Ben enters the bar, a little unsteadily.

JIM [*with a smile that gives a fleeting youth to his face*]: Hello, Ben—you're late.

[*Ben sits down without speaking. Jim takes out a large watch.*]

JIM: You're eighteen minutes late, Ben. Punctuality is the courtesy of kings.

BEN: I'm not a king.

JIM [*wearily*]: Every man is a king—of a private kingdom. You look tired, Ben.

[*Ben nods slightly.*]

Hot day, awful hot. You're lucky you got that cooling system up at Continental. We don't have a dog-gone thing but those old-fashioned ceiling fans. Park Commissioner says in the paper the drought has killed sixteen of the Japanese cherry trees.

BARTENDER [*approaching leisurely*]: Beer?

JIM: Two times twenty-six ounces!

BEN: I don't want beer. Bourbon and seltzer, Mike.

[*The bartender exits.*]

JIM: Huh?

BEN: I stopped and had one on the way. Two, in fact.

JIM: I thought you had a buzz on, the way you came in.

BEN: I did. [*He looks up with a tired grin.*] Eight years ago, Jim, you got me drunk in this place to celebrate our graduation from college.

JIM: Uh-huh.

BEN: What a gloomy celebration! In exchange for our flaming youth we received a piece of parchment, fancy-lettered, tied up in a piece of pale blue satin ribbon. Life is full of phony transactions like that. A young man's dreams, ambitions, the fabulous golden cities of adolescence, sold down the river—for *what*? Eighteen-fifty a week!

JIM: I get twenty-two fifty.

BEN: Three cheers for the plutocrat! Remember the baccalaureate sermon? It was delivered by the Honorable J.T. Faraway Jones, President of the Board of Directors of Continental Shirtmakers. He told me the future was in my hands–Now *I'M* in *his*! [*He tosses down the whiskey, then bangs table with his glass.*] Suds! Suds! Suds! Another twenty-six ounces! Jim—we sat in this very same booth the night of that celebration. This mirror reflected our faces, the same piece of glass. *It* hasn't changed a damned bit–But *we* have, though. *You* used to be *good-looking*!

JIM [*huffily*]: Thank you. So did you—used to be.

BEN: You used to be athletic, an excellent swimmer. Now in your present condition I bet you would drown in the municipal birdbath. Even your eyes have changed color. They used to be blue, energetic. Now they're kind of shifty-looking gray.

JIM [*violently pushing back his chair*]: You've got a nerve to make sarcastic remarks about my personal appearance!

BEN: Don't get hot under the collar.

JIM: Who wouldn't get hot under the collar? Every man of thirty sees himself double in the mirror! The way he looks now—the way he looked at twenty! Nobody has to rub Siberian salt in the wound! And as for you, Mr. Apollo, take a look at yourself. I can't observe a great deal of physical progress.

BEN: I've kept in shape.

JIM: What kind of shape?

BEN: Thrice weekly work-outs in the gym at the downtown Y have preserved my youthful figure. But what I'm driving at is the fact that flesh is not a very durable substance. It's an awfully cheap package in view of what it contains.

JIM: What?

BEN: The wild, incredible fact of being alive!

JIM: Whew!

BEN: It must've been accidental—I mean conscious life. 'Cause surely if they'd planned on it from the start, they would have made a better kind of a box to put it in than this drab stuff we're made of that cracks with the cold and oozes with heat and shows such inordinate lust for disintegration! What do you remember of the time before you were born?

JIM: My recollection of that is kind of cloudy.

BEN: It's on the dark side of the moon. And after you're dead—that's also on the dark side of the moon. But here in the middle—[*He sticks his finger in the center of the table.*] —is one little instant of light—a pin-point of brilliance—right here in the very center of infinite—endless—dark! What are you doing with it? What wonderful use are you making of this one instant?

JIM: I don't like you when you're like this.

BEN: Like what?

JIM: Morbidly profound—the Hamlet of Continental Shirtmakers.

BEN: Yep. I've seen my father's ghost. But he walked at noon and he told me that something was rotten in more than *Denmark*.

JIM: What's happened? A run-in with Gum?

BEN: Yeah.

JIM: For Chrissakes, Ben—he didn't give you the sack?

BEN: Well—he held it toward me. He gave me twenty-four hours—from noon today till noon tomorrow—while he considers my case and makes up his mind whether or not he's going to rip me out of this cozy little cocoon of a job I've snuggled down in for the past eight years. [*He rises and swallows his beer.*] So—for just that little space of eternity, Jim, I'm a man that's suspended in between two lives—*with* a job and with*out* a job! What do you think of that?

JIM: Look here, Ben you're a man with responsibilities. Alma your wife—!

BEN: Yes, Alma, my wife— Once a delectable female, now a *fiend.*

JIM [*rising*]: Ben, you're off your nut!

BEN: Maybe I am, I've had a violent shock. Mentally I'm a submarine brought to the surface for the first time in eight years by the explosion of a terrible depth bomb. Something is going to happen to me tonight.

JIM: *What?*

BEN: I don't *know* what. —So long! [*He grins, salutes and rushes out of the bar.*]

JIM: Ben!

[*Jim starts to follow—but Ben does not wait for him. Jim stops short—catches a glimpse of himself in the mirror. He advances to the tactless declaration of his image. He puts on his glasses, makes a gloomy inspection. "Hmmmm!" He turns this way and that way, trying to draw up his chest. Bertha steps blithely out of the ladies' room and goes straight up to the disconsolate employee of the Olympic Light and Gas Company.*]

BERTHA: Have you got change for a quarter? I want to play something.

JIM [*welcoming her like springtime*]: You bet I have! What shall we hear?

BERTHA: Something about the moon and the South Sea Islands!

JIM: Personally I prefer the Arctic Circle! [*He inserts a nickel, releasing the tender sadness of steel guitars.*] Right now my libido is concentrating on Eskimo girls—with icicle ornaments on them! A necklace of Frigidaire cubes—more dazzling than diamonds! Would you care to dance with a man who used to be handsome?

[*They dance.*]

BLACKOUT

SCENE FOUR

"BLUE HEAVEN"

The stage is dark. There is a musical interlude: a satirical treatment of Irving Berlin's "Blue Heaven" with twittering bird-notes, etc. A blue spot lights a double bed with a stout woman on it, Ben's wife, Alma. Her face is glittering with cold cream, and her hair is done up in wire curlers. She is a woman corresponding to the spider of a certain species that devours her mate when he has served his procreative function.

In the hall off stage a cuckoo clock begins to strike the hour. Alma sits up in bed and listens attentively.

There is the sound of a cautious entrance. The bedroom door opens a crack and spills light from the hall.

A cat screeches with diabolical vehemence.

ALMA [*furiously*]: What didja do? Step on 'er?

BEN: No!

ALMA: She wouldn't have screeched like that unless she was hurt.

BEN: She's just got it in for me, that's all.

ALMA: If she's got it in for you, it's because you do 'er some kind of deliberate injury every chance you get. Where have you been? Out drinking?

BEN: I was out with Jim.

ALMA: That answers the question. How much beer did you drink?

BEN: Three times twenty-six ounces, whatever that makes.

ALMA: I thought we decided to put your beer money up for the baby's carriage.

BEN: Man proposes—God disposes, Alma.

ALMA: All right. We'll just put the baby on roller skates I suppose. Mother just got off the phone.

BEN: Was she on the phone?

ALMA: She thinks it's absolutely outrageous.

BEN: What does she think is outrageous?

ALMA: You know what. I waited for you one solid hour. I made th' spaghetti dish. I kept it hot in the oven till nearly seven and then I ate it myself, ev'ry scrap of it, too. I said to Mother, "Why should I keep his food for 'im? He don't come home or even call th' house." "If Ben makes yuh nervous," she said, "just pack up yuh things an' come home; in your condition you can't afford t' be nervous!"

[*Ben has undressed in the dark. He collapses on the bed in his shorts.*]

I guess we ought to have twin beds in the summer. Stay on your own side, please.

BEN: Don't worry, Alma. I'm going to stay on my side.

ALMA: I been to the doctor's. Dr. Robertson is a lovely young man. He has a beautiful respect for motherhood. He said, "Mrs. Murphy, you're doing a wonderful thing. You're going to bring a brand-new life into the world!"

BEN: Yeah. I guess that's right.

ALMA: A miraculous thing is what Dr. Robertson called it.

BEN: Alma, what right have I got to have a baby?

ALMA: None whatsoever. But nature is lenient, Ben, and she's giving you one. Now you're becoming a father you'll have to settle down.

BEN: Settle down, huh? What have I been doing the last eight years? Stirring up?

ALMA: Yes. Stirring up hell in general for me and all my relations. Go to sleep.

BEN: You women are too easy-going.

ALMA: What do you mean by that crack?

BEN: Before you let a man be the father of your children you ought to demand that he should do something to improve the world that the kid has to grow up in. Me, for instance. What have I done to improve the world?

ALMA: Nothing!

BEN: Then I shouldn't be allowed to reproduce. But you women are so easy-going a man can come to you with nothing but the ordinary equipment and you'll shout welcome so loud that the windows will break in all the adjacent buildings.

ALMA: That's disgusting and it isn't true.

BEN: It is. You think that anything that coos and gurgles and slobbers over your breast is perfectly good enough to populate the earth with. Race improvement? Why should you bother with it! Candy manufacturers are more discriminating. At least they have pure food laws. Some standards of quality in their product. But you, you produce a congenital moron and shout to the world, "Thank God I've got a baby!" Miraculous is what Dr. Robertson calls it. What happens? The kid grows up and works for Consolidated something or other. His lungs shrivel up from artificial ventilation and his eyes get squinted and dull from peering at books all the time with 2-6-8 scribbled on them. What does 2-6-8 have to do with his "miraculous existence"? Not a goddamn thing. But most of his waking hours are 2-6-8, 2-6-8, 2-6-8 —As though those numbers were the combination to the safety vault that God Almighty keeps the mysteries of the universe locked in!

ALMA: Oh, Ben, hush up.

BEN [*in a desperate, rising mutter*]: Colored checks, broadcloth, stripes, madras, mercerized, pre-shrunk, washable, tab, plain, fabric, color size! Oh, God, please eliminate shirts!

ALMA: What are you doing?

BEN: Saying my prayers.

ALMA: Ben—something has happened down at the office today! Hasn't it, Ben?

BEN: Naw.

ALMA: Ben, you're lying! Listen here, Ben, if you throw up this job, I'm going to quit you, I'm going to quit you so fast it will make your fool head swim!

BEN [*suddenly sitting up*]: You know what the earth is, Alma?

ALMA: Ben, have you been discharged?

BEN: A wheel that turns! In a great big gambling casino!

ALMA: Answer me, Ben! Were you discharged at the office?

BEN: Today is the odd, tomorrow will be the even. Tonight is the black, morning will be the red. Which are we going to stop on?

ALMA: Ben! I know you were fired! Fired—weren't you?

BEN: Which are you going to stop on, Alma?

ALMA: Get out of my way. I'm going to call up Mother.

BEN [*backing toward the door*]: The wheel is set in motion, the solar system, around and around it goes!

ALMA: Fired? Yes, fired!

BEN: The whole universe—a great big gambling casino!

ALMA: Lost your mind! Lost your job!

[*He backs out the door, then slams it shut.*]

Fired! I'm going to call Mother!

[*Ben throws the door open and seizes his clothes.*]

BEN: My pants! [*He goes out again, reslamming the door.*]

ALMA [*with consummate disgust*]: His pants!

BLACKOUT

[*Mr. E laughs offstage.*]

SCENE FIVE

"AN ACCIDENT OF ATOMS"

At first the stage is pitch black and soundless. Then, distantly, we hear the hollow echo of footsteps on stone. Gradually, against the cyclorama, are projected the Gothic outlines of a university quadrangle. A spot of ghostly lights falls on a heroic statue of an athlete bearing a torch, on the marble pediment of which is chiseled the inscription "Youth." A small stone bench is beneath it with a graduate's tasseled cap.

Ben steps into the spot of light—he looks gravely up at the statue and takes a drink from a pint bottle of whiskey. He bows to the statue and offers him the bottle.

BEN: Aw, I forgot, You mustn't break training rules—the coach wouldn't like it. Beautiful, shining, clean-minded, clean-limbed American youth—I salute you! [*He sits on the bench.*]

[*Distant singing is heard. Ghostly voices become audible: fragments of lectures remembered, the finely distilled wisdom and passion of seers and poets with which the modern young mind is tempered for the world that blows it to pieces.*]

VOICES: —We, the living, exist in a sliding moment of time which is called reality. What is reality? Does anyone know? —Every theoretical model of the universe beginning with Einstein's, has made the radius of the universe thousands of times greater than that part now visible. —One hundred thousand times ten thousand light years is a billion light years, a distance that would stretch across the whole universe now visible to astronomers. —Ah, but we live in an *expanding* universe, a universe that exhibits a mysterious passion for growth! —Yes. It would stagger the imagination to conceive of what may ultimately become the full extent of things described by that important little verb "to be." Indeed it would be impossible for thought to evolve a figure sufficiently huge—

31

[*Ben claps his forehead and leans back against the stone pediment of the statue. There is a sudden crash of brass and roll of drums. Silence. Then a distant choral singing. Pause. Pale blue spectral light appears in the Gothic archway nearby. Into this radiance of recollection steps the lovely, slender figure of a girl in a senior's robe.*]

HELEN: Ben—

BEN: Yes, Helen.

HELEN: I couldn't sleep last night. I had pinwheels in my head. I guess I shouldn't have taken up astronomy this spring. It makes the universe too big and the world too little. It *is* a little world, isn't it? It seems to be so terribly tiny and lost in all of that time and space they say it's surrounded by. And yet— [*She delicately touches her temples.*] On this little star, as they say, by some miraculous accident of atoms—life was created and consciousness occurred and here I am, Ben Murphy, and there you are— [*She stretches out her hands and curves her fingers as though she were clasping his head. Tender wordless singing is heard.*] In this dear, funny little head of yours there's something that holds the image of everything else there is! Holds it until it breaks and then lets it go . . . O Ben, catch me, Ben, I feel dizzy! [*She smiles and closes her eyes.*] I know a lot more than you do about some things. Perhaps I ought to undertake your instruction. Shall I?

BEN [*huskily*]: Yes.

HELEN: In kissing, for instance, there's two kinds of kisses. *This* kind, pure and simple and satisfactory enough for kids coming home from the movies— But then there's another—

BEN: Which is the other, Helen?

HELEN: You'd like me to show you?

BEN: Yeah.

HELEN [*leaning provocatively against the column*]: Hold me close and open your lips when you kiss me!

[*The lights fade out in the archway and Helen disappears. Pause. The choral singing swells in rapture and fades.*]

THE WHISPERING GHOSTLY VOICES AGAIN: Light is not straight but curved. This discovery led to entirely new conceptions of— It being possible, now to determine the weight of an atom— Arrived eventually at the Straits of Magellan! —Silent upon a peak in Darien!* —Latitude! Longitude! —East by West! — Island! Indies! Archipelago! Hesperides! —It is blood to remember; it is fire—to stammer back. —It is God—your namelessness. —Windswept guitars on lonely decks forever!**

[*A spot captures Jim in the archway wearing a varsity sweater. A steel guitar plays "Song of the Islands" faintly.*]

JIM: Aw, quit goofing off!

BEN: You don't know Helen?

JIM: Sure. She writes lyric verse. The perfume in the poison cup. I tell you, Ben, it's instinct with the female to feather the nest. Marry her and you'd spend the rest of your life collecting feathers. Is that what you want?

BEN: Christ! What *do* I want?

JIM: Adventure, excitement! Look! Soon as we graduate we're going to ship out on a cargo boat for Cairo—Shanghai—Bombay!

---

* John Keats, "On First Looking into Chapman's Homer."

** Hart Crane, "The Southern Cross," from *The Bridge*.

We'll survive shipwrecks and write the vivid details of native uprisings. We'll be the calm observers of revolutions or maybe foment them ourselves—our lives will be legendary! Which is preferable, such a life as that or a life that is lived behind a pair of white lace curtains with that little bush-league Edna St. Vincent Millay?

BEN [*frenzied*]: I don't know, I don't know—I can't think. There are so many possibilities—

JIM: *Infinite* possibilities! That's what I've been trying to tell you, you fool! You want to toss 'em all over—for *sex* and a *sonnet*!

[*The spot on Jim fades. A Glee Club is heard singing* Alma Mater.]

COMMENCEMENT SPEAKER: You graduates of the class of 1934 are presented with an unusual challenge. You are being sent out as a stream of revitalizing blood to the world that is dying slowly of spiritual anemia. A world exhausted by recent war, already rearming itself for another. Gripped by unparalleled economic depression for which only the barest experiments are offered for correction. Therefore I say we look to you with an almost frantic appeal—give us new life, you young ones, new courage and new ideas! Build us a brand new faith to revive our spirits!

[*Fade out. Applause. A band starts up. A spot comes up on Jim in cap and gown, lighting a pipe in the archway.*]

BEN: J.T. Faraway Jones came up and congratulated me on my valedictorian address.

JIM: Yeah? Isn't he the president or something of Consolidated Shirtmakers?

BEN: Yep. He wants to give me a job in that colossal sweatshop of his.

JIM: That's a mighty solid corporation. You'd better take it.

BEN: You're not serious, are you?

JIM: Yep. Perfectly serious. One out of ten guys in our class has got the barest possibility of finding any kind of a job.

BEN: How about that cargo boat we were going to ship out on?

JIM: What are your capital assets?

BEN: Eighty-five cents.

JIM: Not quite enough to pay for your passport, sonny. We've got to accumulate a little more money than that before we sail into the sunrise. As a matter of fact, I've taken a job myself—handling complaints down at the Olympic Light and Gas Company.

BEN: Oh. That was a fine speech you made to me when I wanted to marry Helen. Remember? I was sacrificing a life of adventure and excitement for the life of a petty wage earner behind a pair of white lace curtains.

JIM: Don't get me wrong. I'm only taking this job for three or four months.

[*The spot on Jim begins to fade.*]

BEN [*bitterly*]: Three or four *years*—five years—six years— seven—eight! You cheat! You phony! You coward! You dirty liar! [*He hurls the empty whiskey bottle at Jim's now vanishing figure. It shatters upon the stone archway. Then hoarsely and brokenly:*]

35

"O, Harry—Thou hast robb'd me of my youth!"*

[*Distant choral singing is heard. High in the Gothic tower above the quadrangle the bells begin to chime the midnight hour. Ben turns slowly back to the exalted statue of youth. He raises his arms in a baffled, imploring gesture. But the bells ring on, slowly and obliviously. He drops his arms—falls sobbing against the marble pediment of the statue. Footsteps ring along the stone. The singing comes up stronger and clearer. A Youth in military uniform appears. Ben turns to face him. The Youth salutes and starts to pass by.*]

Hey!

[*The Youth pauses with a smile. Ben continues, extending the tasseled cap.*]

Is this yours?

YOUTH: It *was*. But I have a *new* one. [*He touches the visor of his cap.*]

BEN [*slowly and bitterly*]: You have in your body about three gallons of blood. Is that enough to wash the world's dirty hands?

YOUTH: How do I know? Maybe it is and maybe it isn't. So long. [*He smiles brightly and strangely and passes out of sight.*]

[*The light fades and the music fades.*]

BLACKOUT

[*Mr. E sighs offstage.*]

---

* *Henry IV: Part One, Act V, Scene IV,* Hotspur.

"WHITE LACE CURTAINS"

A spot comes up on the corner of the living room in Jim's bunga-low on Peach Street—or is it Elm? White lace curtains are at a window; there is a ridiculously large and ornate radio-Victrola with a goldfish bowl on top. On the wall above the radio is a pic-ture of "Hope" seated blindfolded and playing a broken-stringed lyre. Jim is seated beside the radio-Victrola with a glass of ice water. He has on purple pongee pajamas with white-frogged but-tonholes.

His wife Edna calls from offstage.

EDNA: Jim!

JIM: Yep.

EDNA: Comin' t' bed?

JIM: Soon as I cool off a little. I'm worried about Ben Murphy. I'm afraid he's going to pieces.

EDNA: Ben has always been an absolute screwball. Even his wife admits it. She told me yesterday that he's been going down to the office in cowboy boots! Confidentially, she said, I'm just about through!

JIM: He's plunging back into his adolescence. Talks about rebel-lion. Rebellion is all right for the upper classes and the lower class-es, but for the middle classes—it will never do! The middle has always got to be the middle.

EDNA: Please close the bedroom door and talk the whole thing over with yourself.

JIM [*wearily*]: Okay, sweetheart. [*He steps out of the spot and can be heard closing the door. He returns and switches on the radio.*]

H. V. KALTENBORN*: Was described as being in a sea of flames: Very little damage was done to military objectives but the civilian population suffered terrible casualties. The sky at midnight was a blazing inferno. Wave after wave of dive bombers swooped down upon the already blasted metropolis. The whole residential section was laid to waste. Helpless women and children by the tens of thousands—

[*Jim casually switches the dial.*]

BABY-TALK SINGER: But this little piggy was a *bad* little piggy
                And he boogie-woogied all the way home!

[*The doorbell rings. Jim turns off the radio and moves out of the spot. He can be heard admitting the caller—Ben.*]

JIM: Aw, *you* again.

BEN: Yeah. Me again.

[*They step into the spot. Ben's appearance is completely demonic.*]

EDNA [*sharply*]: Who on earth was that ringing the doorbell at this time of night?

JIM [*puts finger to lips*]: Nobody, sweetheart. Go to sleep.

EDNA: Nobody? Awwwww! —You mean Mr. Benjamin Murphy!

---

* American news commentator for CBS and NBC; famed for his frontline radio broadcasts during World War II.

BEN [*sorrowfully*]: What a dreadful bitch that woman is.

JIM: Shhh! Sit down.

BEN: It's hot as blazes in here.

JIM: Edna's got the fan.

BEN: So has Alma.

JIM: Why are you barging in here at this time of night?

BEN: Partly to ask your pardon for what I said at Mike's. I didn't mean to be nasty about your appearance.

JIM: Oh, well. I'm not self-conscious. Besides—

BEN: Huh?

JIM: I recognized a certain amount of truth in some of your statements.

BEN: Did you?

JIM: Yes.

BEN: Which ones? About your loss of resistance?

[*Jim nods slowly.*]

Then what'll you do about it?

JIM: Nothing.

BEN: You'll do nothing?

[*Jim nods.*]

Nothing at all?

JIM: What *can* I do?

BEN: Resist it!

JIM: Resist what? How?

BEN: In fighting gangrene they cut off the affected members.

JIM: Okay. Give me an axe and I'll cut off my head.

BEN: You don't have to cut off your head.

JIM: What, then?

BEN: The superfluous fat on your spirit. The weekly paycheck that corrupted a marathon swimmer.

JIM: Shylock! —What did you lend me?

BEN: Belief! —Once. Don't you remember?

JIM [*with a mocking lilt*]: "Sweet Alice—Ben Bolt."

BEN: I took a walk just now around the campus.

JIM: That must've been gruesome.

BEN: It was. I talked with a number of ghosts, including yours.

JIM: What did mine have to say?

BEN: A lot of what turned out to be the sort of stuff they remove from stable floors with a shovel. I wanted to marry a girl who wrote lyric verse. No, wait, you said, don't give up infinite possibilities for sex and a sonnet. Don't live out your life behind a pair of white lace curtains. Well, I got the sex all right, but without the sonnet. Here's the white lace curtains in your window. A duplicate pair's in mine. What happened to the tramp steamer in which we were going to ship out? [*Pause.*]

JIM [*somberly*]: Scuttled.

BEN: Yeah. Scuttled. Once you asked life a question. You got no answer. Instead of grabbing a pick and shovel and tearing into the Sphinx to force the oracle out, you lay down flat in front of her in the hot desert sun and went to sleep with your shirt pulled over your head. [*Pause.*]

JIM [*wearily*]: Define the issues.

BEN: You know what they are.

JIM: Vaguely.

BEN: Vagueness is what makes sheep of populations! Haven't we learned we can't be sheep any more now that we know that sheep are merely kept to be *shorn*—and *slaughtered*? I want to refurnish my life!

JIM: With what?

BEN: New things! *Beliefs*—that are like steel weapons! *Ideals*—that catch the sunlight!

JIM: Where will you find them? In what political party?

BEN: In the political party of my heart! In my instinct that tells me I don't have to be caged!

JIM [*quietly with dignity*]: Ben, I'm just as hungry for things to believe in as you are. I used to have social convictions even before you had them. What happened? I saw how little they meant to the people I got them from. I'm human, I'm disillusioned—I need a new faith. Find me a new faith, Ben. Do that and I'll face round about. I'll cut off this comfortable fat that offends your eye. I'll sell my belongings, quit my wife, and my job, and enlist in the new Crusade! But not until you've produced the *corpus delicti*—Ben, you're not a genius, my lad, and neither am I. We belong to the class of wage earners—the little people—made for normal adjustments!

BEN: Bungalows on Peach Street?

JIM: Yes.

BEN: Faded purple pajamas?

JIM: Yes.

BEN: White lace curtains?

JIM: Yes.

BEN: *NO!* [*He seizes the white lace curtains and tears them down.*]

JIM [*gently*]: A stupid gesture, a useless act of resistance. Edna, my wife, will put them back up tomorrow.

[*Ben catches his breath in a desperate sob. He looks about wildly, then charges out. The door is heard slamming.*]

EDNA [*wildly at the telephone*]: Alma? Alma, that screwball husband of yours is over here raising the roof and I just can't endure it! —Huh?

JIM: Ben's gone, Edna. [*Pause.*]

EDNA: I just called Alma. —She's all packed up and is going home to her mother. —Now what would you call that?

JIM: The luck of the Irish!

FADE

[*Mr. E laughs offstage.*]

"THE LETTER"

A spot lights a bed in a rooming house. On the edge of it the Girl is seated forlornly in pajamas. Bertha, her roommate, enters.

BERTHA: Still up? —Why didn't you meet me at Mike's?

GIRL: I didn't feel able to.

BERTHA: You missed it! Romance came into my life with a bang, but the man was married. [*She sits on the bed to remove her shoes.*] Married to a woman named Edna who massages her chest with Vick's Vapo-Rub every night. You look sort of down in the mouth. What's the matter? [*She removes her stockings.*] Still holding the torch for Mr. Warren B. Thatcher?

GIRL: I'm desperate, Bertha.

BERTHA: Forget it. Just let it all go. Drop it like you would a piece of loose thread. Say to yourself tonight as you go to sleep, "Tomorrow I won't think about him."

GIRL: Why should I lie to myself when I know that I will? Besides—there won't be any tomorrow.

BERTHA: You know what you ought to do? Go to church, read a book, learn how to play contract bridge.

GIRL: You don't understand.

BERTHA: Don't you think I ever had a crush?

GIRL: This man isn't a crush.

BERTHA: What would you call it, then?

GIRL: Love.

BERTHA: Because he's your boss and he wears a white linen suit and a pale blue tie every day, you think you're in love.

GIRL: Oh, Bertha. [*She stands.*] Bertha, am I invisible?

BERTHA: What an idea!

GIRL: Nobody seems to notice me, nobody seems to be conscious of my existence!

BERTHA: Men, you mean? Don't be discouraged. For every surprise there happen to be at least fifteen disappointments. And nowadays men are concentrating on war at the cost of sex. What of it. Your day will come! How would you like a bromide?

GIRL: No, thanks.

BERTHA: I had another girlfriend kept brooding over some man that worked at her office. He never looked at her even. Drop it, I said, "like you would a piece of loose thread." She wouldn't take my advice. "Willard," she said, "Willard, Willard"! —That was his name. —You know what she finally did?

GIRL: Killed herself?

BERTHA: No. Went into *dementia praecox*, I couldn't stop her. Insulin shock couldn't save her.

GIRL: I've done something awful.

BERTHA: What?

GIRL: Oh, I can't tell you! I wrote him a letter!

BERTHA: Come on! What awful thing? Mr. Warren B. Thatcher?

GIRL: Yes!

BERTHA: Did you mail it?

GIRL: I left it on his desk. He'd already gone for the afternoon.

BERTHA: What did you write Mr. Thatcher?

GIRL: I wrote him I loved him.

BERTHA: Oh. —You come right out with it, huh?

[*The Girl covers her face. Pause.*]

Honey, get into yuh things.

GIRL: Get on my things?

BERTHA: Yeah, get dressed!

GIRL: What for?

BERTHA: You're going down to that office and pick up that letter before Mr. Thatcher sees it.

GIRL: The building's closed.

BERTHA: Wake up the night watchman, baby, an' get that letter! You take it from me it would be an awful mistake for him to read it! I made a confession like that to a boss once myself, and, boy, oh, boy, was I *unem*ployed the next morning! Get into yuh things, sweetheart. —Be quick about it!

GIRL: But, Bertha—

BERTHA: Yeah?

GIRL: What I said in the letter was *true*!

BERTHA: Never mind that. That's strictly incidental.

GIRL: I *do* love him!

BERTHA: Get into yuh things—yuh hear me?

GIRL: Yes, I will, I will— But that doesn't solve any problems! I'm desperate, Bertha.

BERTHA: Well, all I can say is, it's better to be desperate with a job than desperate without one. —Here's your— [*She throws the Girl's underwear at her.*]

BLACKOUT

[*Mr. E laughs offstage.*]

SCENE EIGHT

"DID SOMEBODY CALL THE NIGHT WATCHMAN?"

The lights come up on a downtown corner at midnight. On the corner stands Continental Shirtmakers, the sixteen-story shaft (projected on the backdrop) dwindles skywards in exaggerated perspective. Around it are similar shafts, a maze of buildings. Cold and glacial in their appearance at midnight—sharp as knives they ward off the softness of heaven. They bristle defensively shrieking "Stay back!" to God.

A ghostly music is heard.

The Girl appears, tiny, gnat-like among these giants of stone. She stares up at them in wonder and fear and confusion. Hastily, timidly, she runs up to the portal of Continental Shirtmakers.

GIRL [*crying plaintively*]: Night watchman! Oh, night watchman!

[*There is a hollow echo among the walls of stone. She continues desperately.*]

Night watchman, night watchman, night watchman!

[*An echo is heard away in the distance. A uniformed policeman steps around the corner and strikes his stick.*]

OFFICER: What do you want, young lady?

GIRL: I want to get into that building.

OFFICER: This building's closed. It won't be open till morning.

GIRL: If I could get the night watchman's attention I think he might let me in.

OFFICER: The night watchman's deaf.

GIRL: Deaf?

OFFICER: Yes, deaf as stone! He won't hear you! He's also blind as a bat.

GIRL: Then how can he watch?

OFFICER: He can't.

GIRL: What'll I do?

OFFICER: Go home and sleep like other respectable ladies.

GIRL: I can't sleep.

OFFICER: You have something on your conscience?

GIRL: Yes.

OFFICER: What?

GIRL: A letter. I wrote a letter.

OFFICER: What kind of a letter?

GIRL: A love letter. It's locked in that building. I've got to get it back before he reads it.

OFFICER: I never heard of a love letter being written inside that building before.

GIRL: Well, now you've heard of it, though. I'll come back after a while and try again.

[*She moves sadly and tiredly around the corner. . . .Ghostly music is heard. . . . Ben Murphy appears in cowboy boots and a broad-brimmed dove-gray Stetson, several drinks under his emerald-studded belt.*]

OFFICER: Hi, there, cowboy!

BEN: Howdy, Sheriff! I wanted to see how this place looks at night. Romantic, huh? Very, very romantic! Oh—I wanted to ask you a question. How do I get out?

OFFICER: Out of what?

BEN: The cage, the universal cage—The Cage of the Universe! When you were in kindergarten didn't you play with blocks?

OFFICER: Hey, now, look here, if you—!

BEN: Didn't you have a set of alphabet blocks—a nest of blocks, they called 'em? One was big and it fitted over another slightly smaller, and one was slightly smaller than that one and fitted under that one, and still another was slightly smaller still and fitted under—under—under—*ad infinitum*?

OFFICER [*after a pause*]: Odd is right. —But I don't know about "infinitum."

BEN: Officer, what I'm looking for is the very top box, the biggest box of them all, the one that fits on top of all the others! If I can find it, maybe I, with a little mouse-like gnawing, can wriggle out—and be the first and original *HOMO EMANCIPATUS*! Meaning—COMPLETELY FREE MAN! Isn't that a beautiful ambition?

OFFICER: Yep. Yep, very beautiful. Where do you live?

BEN: Nowhere *now*. —Good night. [*He salutes tipsily and runs around the corner.*]

[*The Officer grunts and moves in the other direction. The ghostly music is heard again. A drunken derelict with a beautiful tenor voice passes along the street singing "I Wonder What's Become of Sally!" The Girl re-appears. She shrinks against the wall as the vagrant passes.*]

VAGRANT [*pausing*]: Are you Sally?

[*The Girl shakes her head, frightened.*]

Pardon me—I just wondered. [*He resumes his song and wanders around the corner.*]

GIRL [*crosses to the door and calls*]: Night watchman? Oh, night watchman!

[*Ben comes back around the corner. He pauses in front of the door and strikes a match. The Girl utters a loud gasp.*]

BEN: Hello.

GIRL [*after a pause, timidly*]: —Heh—lo.

BEN: You sound a bit nervous.

GIRL: I am.

BEN: Not about me, I hope. —I'm just a night prowler.

GIRL: A what?

BEN: A night prowler. A man that prowls at night.

GIRL: That isn't a very—reassuring—statement.

BEN: Don't let it alarm you, lady. There's two kinds of night prowlers, malignant and benign.

GIRL: Which are you?

BEN: Benign. Extremely benign.

GIRL: That's good.

BEN: What's your trouble, Miss?

GIRL: I left a letter in this building and I want to get it out before daybreak, but the night watchman's deaf; he can't hear me.

BEN: What kind of a letter was it?

GIRL: An indiscreet one.

BEN: All good literature's an indiscretion. Do you work in this building?

GIRL: Yes.

BEN: So do I. You ever go up to the roof?

GIRL: No. Can you?

BEN: Sure, there's stairs to the roof.

GIRL: I haven't discovered them yet.

BEN: Nobody has but me. I'm the Christopher Columbus of the Continental roof. Say—in case I don't go up there any more, I'd like you to do something for me. I have some dependents up there.

A beautiful flock of pigeons. They're used to me feeding them every day about noon. I may be called out of town on business and I'd like to leave some trustworthy person in charge.

GIRL: What do you feed them?

BEN: Golden Bantam corn.

GIRL: I'd be very glad to assume that responsibility for you.

BEN: Many thanks. Go as far up as the elevator goes and then keep going. —You'll see a flight of stairs.

GIRL: It sounds exciting.

BEN: Do you like excitement?

GIRL: I haven't had enough of it to know.

BEN: Then come with me and we'll go night-prowling together. We'll make observations in the dark of the moon; we'll penetrate to the very heart of darkness. And when the sun comes up, we'll know all the forbidden secrets; we'll wear the expert grins of the rarest cognoscenti.

GIRL: That's a very tempting invitation.

BEN: You can't afford to decline it.

GIRL: People do lots of things they can't afford to do.

BEN: Such as?

GIRL: Writing letters containing fatal admissions! What's that over there? [*She points to a string of golden lights that are moving across a space between two buildings.*]

BEN: It seems to be a golden wheel in heaven.

GIRL: It seems to be turning!

BEN: Yes.

GIRL: I wonder what it could be?

BEN: Let's investigate, huh?

GIRL: How?

BEN: By walking straight toward it!

GIRL: But that would probably take us across the park.

BEN: What if it does?

GIRL: People have warned me not to walk in the park this time of night.

BEN: What would you have to fear with my protection?

GIRL: You? You're an absolute stranger!

BEN: So are you? What of it! I challenge the best that's in you!

GIRL: What's that?

BEN: Curiosity—courage—the lust for adventure!

GIRL: Isn't that an awful lot to expect of just anybody you happen to meet on a corner?

BEN: You're not just anybody! You're ALICE!

GIRL: Who?

BEN: Alice. The everlasting Alice in every girl's heart! Looking for Wonderland! Isn't that true? Tell me if I'm mistaken!

GIRL: You're not mistaken.

BEN: Okay! —Coming, Alice?

GIRL: Okay! —Coming, Rabbit!

[*She laughs and takes his arm and they go off together. The night watchman, very old and decrepit, steps out of the doorway, holding up his lantern and blinking his sightless eyes.*]

NIGHT WATCHMAN: Did somebody call? Did somebody call the night watchman?

[*Sad, faint, faraway music of the spheres is heard...*]

SLOW BLACKOUT

[*Mr. E laughs softly offstage.*]

"KEYS TO THE CAGES"

A densely wooded section of the city park is suggested by the outline of trees with hanging moss and vines against a dark night sky. The golden wheel is faintly visible through the jungle-like weeds and there is barely audible music.

Ben and the Girl enter, moving uncertainly in the dark.

GIRL: I can't make out a thing, can you?

BEN: Not much. Are you scared?

GIRL: No. It doesn't matter what happens to me.

BEN: Why do you say that?

GIRL: Don't ask me, please. Oh, there's the golden wheel—it's getting closer. I can hear music. I'm beginning to suspect what it is.

BEN: Don't be suspicious. Keep your faith in possibilities, Alice.

GIRL: Where are we now?

BEN: We're near the zoo. I can hear the foxes crying.

GIRL: I wonder what they're crying for?

BEN: The same thing we're crying for. They long for the hills and freedom the same as we do.

GIRL: Someone's coming!

BEN: The keeper. The man with the keys to the cages.

[*A gruff-looking little man closely resembling the night watchman appears with a huge bunch of keys and a lantern.*]

Hello, there, Keeper.

KEEPER [*grunting*]: Kind of late to be visiting the zoo.

BEN: It's never too late to take a look at the foxes.

KEEPER: I don't like to have 'em disturbed this late. They're restless little monsters. One of the females's in the family way and I'm going to take a look at her.

BEN: You mean she's going to have babies in that smelly little cage?

KEEPER: Sure. Where else would she have 'em?

BEN: Out in the woods somewhere would be a lot better.

KEEPER: The feisty little bitch'll have 'em here and like it.

BEN: I suppose you've got the keys to all the cages?

KEEPER: I've got the key to every animal cage in the zoo.

BEN: All marked with tags?

KEEPER: Yep, all marked with tags. —So long.

BEN: Just a minute.

KEEPER: Huh?

[*Ben clips him on the chin and seizes the keys. The Girl screams. Music comes up.*]

BEN [*rapidly sorting the keys*]: Elephants! Tigers! Kangaroos! Flamingos! Ahh, here it is, foxes!

GIRL: What are you going to do?

BEN: I'm starting out on the career of emancipator! Just one minute!

[*He darts out of sight. A steel door is heard clanging open. The excited barking of foxes is heard. Ben comes running back.*]

Come along quick before the keeper comes to!

GIRL: Oh, my heavens, what have you done?

BEN: I let 'em loose!

[*The Keeper sits up.*]

Quick! Follow me! [*They rush off.*]

KEEPER: Hey! My God, the foxes! [*He jumps up and fires two shots in the air.*] Stop, thief! Stop, thief! Help, help! Stop, thief!

[*All the animals in the zoo are awakened, and they all roar at once—the braying of the elephant homesick for the jungle, the lonely roar of the lion, the sorrowful chattering of the little monkeys.*]

FADE

[*Mr. E shakes with laughter offstage.*]

"EVERY GIRL IS ALICE"

Across a wide black lake, willow-fringed, we see the moving lights of the carnival or amusement resort. A faint, ghostly music comes from the carousel.
    Ben and the Girl enter right.

GIRL [*breathlessly*]: Are they still coming after us?

BEN: Quick! Get back of those willows!

[*They crouch behind a canopy of willow leaves. Enter two guards from the zoo.*]

ONE: Well, they didn't go no further in this direction.

TWO: I bet they took a short cut over th' links to Wilmington Blvd. You go round that way an' I'll go this.

ONE: Hey! How many foxes was there in that pen?

TWO: Fifteen.

ONE: All of 'em get loose?

TWO: Ev'ry goddamn one of 'em.

ONE [*as they exit*]: Where you reckon they went to?

TWO: Back to the hills they was born in. [*The voices and foot-steps fade.*]

[*The Girl giggles.*]

BEN: Shut up!

[*The Girl giggles louder.*]

SHUT UP!

[*The Girl laughs uncontrollably. Ben shakes her.*]

GIRL: Oww! —I'm all right now. Hadn't we better start running again?

BEN: No, we're better off right here.

GIRL: We can't stay here all night.

BEN: Why can't we?

GIRL: Why—what would my roommate think?

BEN: She'll probably figure that you've been catting around.

[*The Girl steps cautiously out of the willows.*]

GIRL: Oh, look!

BEN [*following*]: What?

GIRL: The lights!

BEN: Yeah, there they are. It's just an amusement park. I warned you it would be something disappointing.

GIRL: I'm not disappointed. You know what it seems like to me? The way the world was when I was a little girl. Beautiful and mysterious and full of lovely music!

BEN: It isn't like that any more.

GIRL: No, but I guess it could be. Under the right circumstances.

BEN: What are the right circumstances?

GIRL: Love, I suppose.

BEN: Is that your Wonderland, Alice? —Love?

GIRL: Uh, huh. Every girl is Alice and love is her Wonderland— But mine seems to be on the other side of the lake and I'm not much of a swimmer. How is the grass? Is it dry?

BEN: Perfectly. Sit down.

[*They sit down at the edge of the lake.*]

GIRL: Oh, my. This is a terribly crazy thing for me to be taking part in. The emancipation of foxes and playing hide-and-seek with mad zoo keepers! Wouldn't my boss have a laugh if he knew about it?!

BEN: What business is it of his? What does your boss have to do with it?

GIRL: Nothing—except that—

BEN: Huh?

GIRL: I'm in *love* with my boss.

[*The carousel starts again with its gay and ghostly music.*]

BEN [*disgustedly moving away*]: Awww.

GIRL [*anxiously*]: What's the matter? Please don't be put out!

BEN: Put out? About what! —I'm just a little bit disillusioned, that's all.

GIRL: Why should you be?

BEN: We meet on a dark street corner. You're cool and white and mysterious. You have a remote and unspecific charm. Where are you from? From away up north somewhere. Not from Minneapolis, not from Chicago, but just from away up north, a place of lakes and cedars and mountains covered with snow. Then, all at once, like a silly jack-in-the-box, your boss projects his ugly head in the picture! A head that looks like an over-ripe tomato!

GIRL: That isn't the way his head looks.

BEN: All right! What does he look like?

GIRL: YOU.

BEN: *What?*

GIRL: You, you, you! He looks very much like you. Don't you remember how I gasped when you struck that match on the corner? I saw your face and the white linen suit and it startled me so that I had to gasp out loud! You know what I thought for a moment?

BEN: What?

GIRL: I thought you were actually *him*!

BEN: Absurd!

GIRL: Isn't it, though? If love could be dignified, it wouldn't be so awful. But it isn't dignified. —At least not for me. —I make a fool of myself. Today for instance he asked me the name of a plaintiff who charged that some weather stripping had not been put in correctly. A man named—Deisseldorff! —You see how fantastic it is? He wanted me to find the correspondence. I couldn't find it.

BEN: Don't you have files in your office?

GIRL: Oh, of course we have files. —But did you ever try to remember the alphabet when you're in love?

BEN: No. How did this dreadful, frustrated passion get started?

GIRL: His secretary got married, he needed another, and I had just completed a three months' course at Rubicam Business College.

BEN: Very exciting. Sounds like the first paragraph of something called "Stolen Moments" in a Macfadden publication. Go on!

GIRL: No, I won't. [*She sobs.*] I'm not asking for sympathy—but I don't need sarcasm, either!

BEN [*taking her hand*]: Forgive me, Alice. Go on— You applied for the job?

GIRL: I applied for the job. I was terribly scared.

BEN: What about?

GIRL: I'm always frightened, it's something organic, I guess. My tongue gets stuck in my throat. —I want to be charming and brilliant—a person who says clever things. —I sit with my teeth in my mouth—as dumb as an owl! —Only afterwards—when I'm alone—I think of what to say! —So when I applied for the job—I lost my voice. I could only speak in a whisper. —He smiled. I got back my courage. —He wanted to know what my typing speed was and he gave me a little dictation. Come back Monday, he said—the position is yours!

BEN: Ahhh!

GIRL: I had on a light pink dress—

BEN: A bad mistake.

GIRL: Yes, it turned out that it was. 'Cause when I got up from the desk—Warren—I mean Mr. Thatcher—he looked up quickly and said, "I'd rather you didn't wear pink. I've got an allergy to pink." That's the only personal thing he ever said to me the whole time I've been employed there.

BEN: Goodness!

GIRL: And just today—I wore the pink dress again.

BEN: Why?

GIRL: Out of sheer desperation! I thought it might force him to look at me and say something personal to me.

BEN: Did he?

GIRL: No, he just frowned a little when I came in the office. You see, he wears a white linen suit—a fresh one every single day of the week—and when I have a pink dress on, I suppose—I suppose he thinks it makes it look a little bit too much like a garden party.

BEN: That is probably what he thinks it makes it look a little bit too much like.

[*Pause. The ghostly music is heard.*]

GIRL: It—wasn't much—at first.

BEN: What wasn't?

GIRL: My love for the boss.

BEN: Oh. But it improved later on?

GIRL: Got worse—and worse.

BEN: I see.

GIRL: At first I only thought to myself—"I like the shape of his head!" It's like a fever—it started out very slowly. Hardly noticeable, you know. A fraction of a degree one day, another fraction the next, till all of the sudden—and just as though you hadn't received any warning—you're literally burning up! You're all on fire. Even your *bones* are melting! Oh, why didn't somebody tell me that things like this are able to happen to people! You know what they ought to have? A sentry outside of life, a man with a big red lantern— A warning bell, gates like at railroad crossings! —With a big sign that says—"*DANGER! LOVE AHEAD!*" That's what they ought to have at the entrance to life. So none but the brave would go forward, and those that are weak or frightened—the way I am—could turn around and go back where it's safe and dark . . .

[*Pause. The song of the carousel is heard again.*]

BEN: Yep, love's a peculiar sickness, I imagine.

GIRL: If I could cry out, if I could scream, if I could make a big scene— It might be some relief.

BEN: You can't?

GIRL: Certainly not. If I did I would lose my job. —You see, Mr. Anonymous—I'm caught in the cage the same as those fifteen foxes!

BEN: Would you like me to conk your boss and steal the keys and let you out of the cage?

GIRL: Oh, if you only could! —But it isn't that easy. I'm afraid that love is one cage that there isn't any way out of. I have to walk back and forth, forth and back with bunches of legal papers on such irrelevant matters as people named Deisseldorff and mysterious odors. —Open the files, shut the files—bang away at those doggone little white keys! Sometimes I want to stop and say to him very, very quietly—"Mr. Thatcher, Mr. Warren B. Thatcher—all of this here—this business, these papers, these files—are against my nature!" Do you think he would understand? No. He'd say, "You're not satisfied?"—and if I said "No," he'd think that I meant with the job.

BEN: If he isn't a fool, he's probably noticed something.

GIRL: He's blind with something—the same as I am.

BEN: What's he blind with?

GIRL: The same thing—love. He's in love with a girl that's married, he calls her up and tells her to meet him tonight at the Cafefree Cabins on Highway 60. When he hangs up, his head bends over the desk, and he broods and groans that civilization's collapsing. I can see the little pink lines of his scalp where his hair's gotten thin and I want so much to stretch out my fingers and touch them, to give him some comfort. —He holds the pencil so tight that it snaps in two! —But I don't dare. —You see how fantastic it is? If something could be very straight—very simple.

BEN: Yeah. Very white—and cool-looking.

GIRL: What a relief it would be!

BEN: Yes. A blessed relief. It would let us out of our cages.

GIRL: But nothing's like that.

BEN: No.

GIRL: It's all tangled up and confused. And the heat of the day is terrific. I went to the priest and said, "Father, I've got to have comfort, I've got to have peace, I've got to have some relief!"

BEN: Did he give you any?

GIRL: No. —Of course not. —How could he? What can I do?

BEN: I don't know.

GIRL: It's hopeless, isn't it? There's no help at all!

[*The faint music of the carousel is heard.*]

BEN: Can't you forget it?

GIRL: That's what my girlfriend says. "Drop it," she says, "like you would a piece of loose thread!" —Oh, God, but I *can't* do that. And I've tried and tried *so* hard.

[*Music comes up. A dim white shape moves leisurely in from the center of the lake. The Girl leans suddenly forward.*]

Oh, my! —What's that? Do you see what I mean? —What's that!

BEN [*rising, softly and distinctly*]: A *swan*.

GIRL [*wonderingly*]: A swan? —Why, yes, so it is! [*She rises and crosses quickly to the very margin of the lake. Coaxingly she stretches out her slim white arm toward the spectral bird. An arpeggio of harp music is heard. The Girl's pose oddly resembles the actual form of the bird.*] Swan! Swan! Beautiful bird, lovely, lovely. —Come closer! Come a little bit closer! Don't be afraid! Give us something very simple! Very white and cool-looking! Be gracious. Be generous to us. We're so hot, so tired and complicated! We have such a terrible fever. Come up closer and make us cool with your beauty.

[*The faint music rises to a rapturous tenderness for a moment, wild arpeggios of harp music—fading, fading, fading! The swan begins to recede upon the smooth black surface of the lake. The Girl continues desperately.*]

Oh! It's moving away! Why is it moving away?

BEN: It isn't domestic—it's wild. It's heard of the cages that tame creatures have built to capture the wild of heart.

GIRL: I don't have a cage.

BEN: Oh, yes, you have—it sees you standing in it.

GIRL: Swan! —It's gone away. The lovely thing's gone away.

[*Ben suddenly kneels beside her at the water's edge.*]

BEN: Oh, no, it hasn't—I have it in my arms! I've caught the swan! [*He embraces her with passion.*] Swan! Swan!

GIRL [*projecting onto him the identity of her loved one*]: Warren!
—Warren, Warren!

BEN: What did you call me?

GIRL [*raptly whispering*]: Warren!

BEN: God. It's a fair transaction! I'll be Warren and you will be the swan!

GIRL: I will, I will dear Warren! —I'm the swan!

[*She leans back rapturously. He presses her slowly to the grass. The carousel goes on and on with its distant, ghostly music as...*]

LIGHTS DIM

[*Mr. E is respectfully silent offstage.*]

SCENE ELEVEN

"THE CARNIVAL-BEAUTY AND THE BEAST"

A carnival occupies a section of the public playgrounds. It is like the set for a rather fantastic ballet as the play progresses further from realism: this may be justified, if necessary, by Ben's increasing intoxication and the exaltation of love in the Girl.

At stage right is a booth containing a perpendicular roulette wheel of a sort, surrounded by the usual assortment of prizes: a beautiful Spanish shawl or mantilla and brilliant cheap jewelry among other articles being touted by the Barker.

Immediately adjoining this is a little box stage with brilliant red and gold silk brocade curtains: the footlights are burning, the curtains closed. Beneath the stage there is a placard that says: PETIT THEATRE PRESENTS "BEAUTY AND THE BEAST." PERFORMANCE: MIDNIGHT.

Above these gorgeously colored little structures, always turning at some distance, the upper half of it visible, is the glittering Ferris wheel which had originally drawn our two protagonists into adventure. The carousel, not visible, can always be heard, however: it has a light repetitive music, somewhat minor—sometimes fast and sometimes slow—with many starts and stops and now and again the distant, indistinct childlike laughter and shouting of the pleasure seekers who ride upon it.

Six or eight people compose the "CROWD" and "AUDIENCE" before the wheel and the stage. They may very well be the same actors as in the office scenes. They wear loud holiday clothes, straw hats with brilliant bands, etc. They are feverishly eager to laugh, desperate for movement, impatient of anything but the trivial distraction: these are the hungry-souled captives of the city let out for a night.

On the real stage, Ben and the Girl are discovered before the gambling concession. Ben is the player and his luck is amazing. Again and again the wheel goes around and he is once more the winner. Under his arms are his winnings: a huge Kewpie doll, a great red stick candy cane, a child's scooter.

The wheel is spinning again.

A broken-hearted Clown enters from left.

CLOWN: Lost, lost! Never to be found again!

[*He holds above a lovely spangled hoop of the kind that is used for jumping trained animals. Everyone ignores him deliberately but the Girl.*]

GIRL [*sympathetically*]: What have you lost?

CLOWN: My little trained dog who used to jump and jump and jump! Right through the middle of this hoop!

GIRL: What happened to him?

CLOWN: He jumped too high and disappeared completely! [*He goes off sobbing, noticed only by the Girl.*]

[*Loud shouts and cheers. Ben has won the gorgeous Spanish shawl. He turns and drapes it about the Girl making her look like one of those resplendent Mexican Madonnas—Our Lady of Guadeloupe. Her momentary sorrow for the clown is gone and she laughs with the others. A trumpet is blown. The curtains divide on the little box stage. A Mummer steps out in a mask and announces:*)

MUMMER: Presenting—"Beauty and the Beast."

[*Two other Mummers appear. One a lovely dark girl in tights and sequins. The other an ugly giant-like creature in the robes of a monk. The backdrop is a medieval castle with a park about it. The First Mummer reads from a scroll as the acting couple perform the little morality play.*]

THE READER: Beauty, who was young and dark and lithe,
   Came on a beast-like creature in her drive.
   She would have passed him but he blocked the way
   And, in the guise of monk, said—

BEAST: Let us pray!

READER: But Beauty, who was young and dark and clever,
   Warily stepped aside and answered—

BEAUTY: Never!

READER: The Beast was *raging*—

[*Aside, the Beast has stage business showing his rage.*]

   But remained polite.
   He gravely bowed to her and said—

BEAST: Good night!

READER: As Beauty passed him, she tossed back her hair,
   And lightly cried—'I leave thee—to thy *prayer*!'

[*Blackout. Brief applause. A placard says* ACT TWO.]

   Next day the Beast again stood in her drive.
   Again she passed him, young and dark and lithe.
   Again he smirked and bowed as she went past,
   But this time *followed*—treading on the grass
   So lightly that his victim heard no sound
   Until he *plunged*—and pressed her to the ground!

[*The above verse is pantomimed by the Actors. Blackout. Hissing. Another placard says* ACT THREE.]

READER [*continuing, before the curtain*]:
   How long she lay with cold, averted face,
   Beneath the Beast, enduring his embrace,
   I cannot say—but when his lust was spent
   And from his veins the scorching fever went—

[*The curtains part again.*]

> He rose above her and was cold as she.
> Then, shivering in equal nudity,
> One faced the other with a speechless look,
> The sky had darkened, now the branches shook—

[*Blue gelatine lights show the Beast standing above Beauty. He has dropped the monk's robe and the ugly mask and is now shown as an austere and handsome young man in pink tights and fig leaf.*]

> A wind sprang up and Beauty was revived,
> She likewise rose and stood upon the drive.
> He was astonished—she was not besmirched.
> Her face was holy as a nun's at church.

[*The erstwhile Beast—business of astonishment and shame, kneeling before her.*]

> She took his hand and whispered—

BEAUTY: Do not grieve—
> I owned no beauty till it felt thy need,
> Which, being answered, makes thee no more Beast,
> But One with Beauty!

READER: Shining as a priest,
> He walked beside her, clinging to her hand
> As cool rain fell upon the fevered land....

[*With the sound of rain and wind, the curtains close on the little stage. Applause. The curtains divide again for the actors to take a bow, but something has gone wrong. The Beast has resumed his ugly mask and is choking Beauty. The Reader flings off his mask and shrieks:*]

Help! Hey Rube!

[*There is a crowd expression of confusion and dismay. Ben, quick-witted, jumps upon the little box stage and feints at the Beast with his candystick cane. With a growl the Beast releases Beauty and advances menacingly toward Ben.*]

Hey Rube! The Beast's gone crazy!

BEN [*feinting with the cane*]: Now, Beast, be reasonable. —Be sensible, Beast. Let's submit the problem to arbitration!

[*But the Beast still advances, growling. Ben continues to the Reader, aside.*]

What nationality is this guy?

READER [*frantic*]: Russian! He don't understand no English! Rube, hey, Rube!

BEN [*suddenly smiling*]: *Tovarishch! Nitchevo, nitchevo! Tovarishch!*[*]

[*Instantly the rampant Beast is changed to a gentle lamb. He purrs and extends his hand to stroke Ben's head. Ben offers him a bite of the cane. He accepts and beams. Cheers. Ben is a public hero. From the crowd there are cries of "Speech! Speech!"*]

Me? A hero? Naa, naw, naw, I'm just a successful linguist! Call any guy a brother in his own language and hostilities are over. Peace is re-established! The peppermint stick is broken in friendship! That, my friends, is the secret of international good fellowship!

---

[*] *Tovarishch*: Comrade; *Nitchevo*: Nothing.

[*This, of course, is interpreted as a plea for appeasement. There is an instant reversal of public opinion. Loud hostile booing follows, together with a shower of popcorn, peanuts and pennies.*]

Okay, okay, I don't know nothin'! I'm just an impractical idealist!

ZOO KEEPER [*shooting off pistol in air*]: He's a *thief*! He just escaped from the zoo with fifteen foxes!

[*He jumps on the box stage pursuing Ben around the Beast. They dodge this way and that.*]

BEAST [*grasping zoo keeper and holding him off*]: Tovarishch?

BEN: No *tovarishch*!

[*The Beast catches the Zoo Keeper under his arm and Ben leaps off the platform and makes a spectacular getaway on the child's scooter won on the wheel. The Girl starts after him but gives up with a cry of despair. The curtains close on the little box stage. The gambling concession is shut down and the lights go out. Quietly, rapidly the crowd disperses. The Ferris wheel stops moving and its lights flicker out; the song of the carousel is slower and fainter and sadder and finally stops altogether. The Girl stands alone in all of this sudden desolation which has the eerie blue atmosphere of a landscape by Salvador Dali. She makes a number of turns and futile gestures. Then in her beautiful shawl she leans broken-heartedly against the closed concession and sobs to herself. From some improbable place Ben suddenly reappears—perhaps he is still on the scooter. He approaches her noiselessly and grins.*]

BEN [*in an altered voice*]: I beg your pardon, lady—do you have a match?

[*Still not recognizing him, the Girl turns slowly and produces a match from her pocketbook and strikes it. In the match light she sees it is Ben and utters a startled cry of relief. They stare at each other silently for a moment. Then with a grateful childlike laugh she nestles into his arms. He continues softly.*]

Tears? Tears? For *me*? You're a woman of miracles, Alice. One moment you're a swan—the next you're a bird of paradise... Now all of a sudden, and most miraculous of all, you're a woman—shedding real honest-to-God tears for me, the first time that has occurred since I came home to Mother with my first black eye some twenty years ago!

[*Back of the curtains on the box, stage music commences again. The Clown comes by joyfully leading his little fox terrier on a brilliantly jeweled collar and chain.*]

CLOWN [*softly and rapturously*]: Found! Found! Never to be lost again!

[*They jingle away offstage. Ben and the Girl embrace. The curtains of the box stage open to reveal Beauty and the Beast—in a ghostly white radiance—locked in a corresponding embrace.*]

CURTAIN

[*Mr. E chuckles offstage.*]

"THIS CORNER'S WHERE WE MET"

The street corner again. A gray light of morning has begun to fil-
ter among the downtown towers.

In the display window of Continental Shirtmakers the Designer
is dressing a dummy. He puts the shirt with the purple dickey and
mother of pearl buttons on him, arranges the arms and torso in a
pose that is very graceful and effete—then stands off to admire his
creation. He sighs and disappears into the interior.

Ben and the Girl appear. The Girl clings to Ben's arms, her eyes
shut, his lips faintly smiling.

BEN: You're walking in your sleep.

GIRL: I thought I must be. I had such a lovely dream. Is it morning?

BEN: Yes. This corner's where we met some time ago.

GIRL: Centuries ago. I didn't know eternity could be so nice!
Poor rabbit! You need a shave. [*She tenderly touches his face.*] I
had no idea you were so funny looking. [*She giggles.*]

BEN [*a little resentfully*]: Funny?

GIRL: Yes, funny and sweet. I like your looks.

BEN: Because I look like your boss?

GIRL: I think I must have forgotten about my boss. He seems to
belong to the year one thousand B.C.! Now there's you and now
there's me, and I'm not looking for apples! [*She hugs him. He*
pushes her gently away.]

BEN: Morning's the time for looking reality square in the face,
you know.

GIRL [*staring at him fondly*]: I'm looking—I'm looking!

BEN: I wonder if you are? I don't believe you know what reality is!

GIRL: Tell me about it. Tell me about reality. I'll believe. Only, when you tell me, hold my hand!

BEN [*taking her hand*]: Reality is composed of some very harsh ingredients, little girl. One of them is the fact I'm out of a job, or almost out of a job. Another one is—I'm married!

GIRL: Oh. [*She turns slowly.*] This is reality—isn't it?

BEN: Yeah. Kind of, I guess. [*Pause.*] Don't be resentful.

GIRL: I'm not.

BEN: Please don't be hurt about anything.

GIRL: I'm not.

BEN: Tonight has been nice, don't you think?

GIRL: Yes.

BEN: We each gave the other something. I gave you Warren. You gave me the swan.

GIRL: You gave more than Warren. You gave me the Wonderland! [*She extends her hand.*] Good-bye!

[*He takes her hand. Then suddenly he embraces her, kissing her roughly. He runs to the corner, turns and makes an odd, awkward salute.*]

BEN: So long, Alice!

[*The Girl starts to wave. He disappears around the corner. The Girl turns slowly, as one who walks in her sleep, and moves in the other direction. The Designer reappears in the window. He makes an ecstatic gesture and embraces the dummy. The music of morning rises amongst the buildings—quick and martial. The day has begun.*]

BLACKOUT

[*Mr. E chuckles offstage.*]

SCENE THIRTEEN

"I'M WORRIED ABOUT MY ROOMMATE"

Scenes Thirteen through Sixteen are sidelights to the main action and should be done in rapid succession by spotting those parts of the stage where action takes place.

A spot lights Bertha talking to her landlady.

BERTHA: Oh, Mrs. Hotchkiss, I'm dreadfully worried about my little roommate! She went out late last night and hasn't come back and I don't where she's gone to!

MRS. HOTCHKISS: She's *probably* gone to the *dogs*!

BLACKOUT

SCENE FOURTEEN

"COME HOME TO MOTHER"

A spot lights Ben's wife at the telephone.

ALMA: Long distance, please. I want to speak to my mother. Hello, Mother? I'm calling from the bus station, I'm going to leave Ben.

[*A spot lights Mother at the other end of proscenium arch at the telephone.*]

MOTHER: What's the trouble, precious?

ALMA: He's lost his mind and he's lost his job and besides I never did like him.

MOTHER: Come home to Mother, darling, come home to Mother!

BLACKOUT

"RISE AND SHINE"

A spot lights Jim's connubial bed, no bed of roses. The alarm clock merrily jangles. Edna sits up, a vision but not *a dream. She roughly shakes Jim out of his slumber.*

HER VOICE [*like a pneumatic drill*]: Rise and shine! Rise and shine! Rise and shine!

JIM [*slowly propping himself up on his elbows.*]: Huh?

EDNA [*still more enthusiastically*]: Rise and shine! Rise and shine! Rise and shine!

[*Jim stares for a moment with absolute incredulity into the face of Edna.*]

JIM [*abysmally groaning*]: MY GOD! [*He flops back down on the bed and covers his face.*]

BLACKOUT

SCENE SIXTEEN

"HELLO AGAIN"

A spot lights Jim advancing from one end of the proscenium arch, Bertha from the other. They stop short recognizing each other. They stare at each other with gentle, wistful smiles. Hawaiian music comes up.

BERTHA: Hello, aren't you the fellow I met at the bar last night?

JIM: That's right. How are you?

BERTHA: I'm all right. Remember the girl that was with me?

JIM: Yeah.

BERTHA: She disappeared.

JIM: That sure is funny. The fellow that I was with has disappeared too. His wife just phoned my wife and told her about it.

BERTHA: What a coincidence, huh? I sure do wish that I could disappear!

[*They both start to walk on. Bertha stops.*]

Hey!

JIM: Huh?

BERTHA: Let's—disappear!

BLACKOUT

SCENE SEVENTEEN

"WHICH CAME FIRST?"

A spot lights Mr. Thatcher's office. He is seated gloomily at his desk.

The Girl enters.

THATCHER [*heavily sarcastic*]: Good morning.

GIRL [*brightly*]: The same to you and many of them, Sir.

THATCHER: If you had arrived exactly nine minutes later I should have had to say good afternoon.

GIRL: Wouldn't that have been awful? May I ask you a question, Mr. Thatcher?

THATCHER: You? Ask *me*? A question?

GIRL: Yes. Me ask you a question. —Which came first in your opinion—Man? Or the clock? Because if the clock came first, then it's only natural, I suppose, that our lives should be regulated by it. But if man came first, then it seems to me that the clock has been taking entirely too much for granted—and ought to be put in its place! [*She lifts the clock from his desk and drops it in the waste basket.*]

THATCHER: What's come over you, Miss—Uh—

GIRL: My name is not Miss Uh! I guess you've read the letter I left on your desk last night.

THATCHER: Yes. I was just going to mention that letter.

GIRL: You needn't. I meant it then, but this morning— Well, everything's different this morning. You see, I spent last night on the shore of a lake. I happened to glance in the water and see my reflection. I'm not ugly, Mr. Thatcher, I'm not a duckling—I'm a snow-white swan. —And from now on I'm going to preen my feathers, I'm going to rustle and glide—and be admired by people! [*She opens the files and pulls out a bunch of papers.*] Look! I'm not butterfingered this morning. See how firmly I can hold these papers? But I don't want to hold them; they're against my nature! [*She tosses them in the air.*] You're always groaning about the collapse of civilization! Do you really believe that civilization's gone?

THATCHER: My last doubt vanished just a moment ago.

GIRL: All right, Mr. Thatcher. But let me tell you this— If civilization is falling, you're not going to walk around gently sighing over the beautiful ruins while we, the little people are lying *squashed underneath*! No, we're going to be on the top of the dump heap, too. And there isn't going to be any gentle sighing about it. There's going to be lots of hard work putting it back together. And the blueprints for the reconstruction are not going to be supplied by the old architects—the ones who put so much water in the cement that it wouldn't hold up! —No! No, we the people, are going to draw them ourselves! Oh! —It's time for lunch!

THATCHER: *What?*

GIRL: Excuse me, I'm going upstairs!

THATCHER: Upstairs?

GIRL: Yes! To the roof, Mr. Thatcher! [*She laughs and goes out.*]

FADE

[*Offstage Mr. E. laughs loud and close by.*]

"UP TO THE ROOF"

The scene is the office of the Continental Branch of Consolidated Shirtmakers. The huge clock indicates it is nearly noon. With piston-like regularity the office force is performing its several functions.

The door of the elevator pops open and out come Mr. P, Mr. D, Mr. Q, and Mr. T, heads of the corporation. Perhaps there has been some kind of national convention. Anyway, each of them has a broad satin band draped over his chest which bears the initials listed above. They seem to be in a terrible state of excitement. They are pursued by the Office Boy who calls out:

OFFICE BOY: Mr. P! D! Q! T! Stocks are tumbling, there's a bear on the market!

P: Never mind that now.

D: We've something more important on our hands!

[*They rush up to Mr. Gum's desk.*]

Q: Gum!

GUM [*rising respectfully*]: Yes, Mr. Q?

Q: A dreadful rumor has just now reached our ears.

P: We understand—

D: That some little clerk in your department—

T: Has discovered stairs to the roof!

Q: Is—this correct?

GUM: Correct!

T: Ahhh, my—

D: Gracious—

P: Me! He'll have to be eliminated—

D: At once!

Q: He possesses knowledge that might very seriously disrupt the affairs of the corporation—

P: If it were indiscriminately passed around!

Q: Who is this man?

GUM: Benjamin D. Murphy.

P: Get him out, fire him, give him his notice this minute!

Q: Wait, wait, wait! Aren't you being a little bit obtuse? Fire Mr. Murphy and he'll be out of our hands. What's to prevent him, then, from telling them *all* about the stairs to the roof? I have a counter-proposal. Offer him something attractive enough to make it worth his while to be—discreet!

D: Q's right.

P: Gum, do you know this man?

GUM: He's been an employee of Continental Branch of Consolidated Shirtmakers for the past eight years.

Q: What kind of proposition would appeal to Mr. Murphy?

GUM: I can't say for certain. I judge him to be a man who longs for movement.

Q: The road?

P: The road, the road!

Q: Put him on the road, as far away from the office as you can get him!

GUM: He mentioned some fond remembrance of Arizona.

Q: Arizona!

P: Perfect! Nothing but Indians!

GUM: Of course, I can't give you any definite assurance that Benjamin D. Murphy is going to be interested in any kind of proposal, however beguiling, whose object is to obstruct what he considers to be the forward and upward will of the human spirit.

Q: Hmmmm. What kind of a man is this Murphy?

GUM: Did you ever read Oliver Twist?

Q: Ahh. An orphan?

P: With criminal tendencies?

GUM: An orphan, gentlemen, who is not satisfied with one bowl full of soup but walks straight up to the astonished Beadle and asks for more! "More?" says the astonished Beadle.

Q: He didn't *get* any more.

P: No, I *remember* the story. He didn't get any more. He walked with his empty soup bowl back to the table and the table was bare!

GUM: But that's where the difference begins. Benjamin Murphy does not return to the bare table with the empty soup bowl. He squares right up to the astonished Beadle and says—"*Yes! More!*"

Q: I always knew that the book was the wrong sort of reading for impressionable young minds. Where is he?

P: Yes, where *is* this latest edition of the dauntless orphan?

GUM: Undoubtedly he's up there on the roof this minute.

Q: Fetch him!

P: Go up there and acquaint him with our proposition!

GUM: Gentlemen, you forget that I'm a good "company" man. What do I know about the stairs to the roof? Where are they, P? D? Q? T?

Q: Gentlemen! —We must search for the stairs to the roof!

[*There is a roll of drums.*]

FADE

[*Mr. E laughs very close by offstage.*]

SCENE NINETEEN

"THE ROOF? WHAT ROOF?"

The roof.

This is the roof of a city office building. But is it actually the roof? Everything points upward like so many fingers that say "In that direction!" We have the sky (as blue as you can make it), the tops of various white stone towers, a few little lamb's wool clouds. The towers have fluttering pennants with curious symbols and glittering weathervanes on them. Below this region the world may be grooved repetition, but here it is the transcendental—Light, light, light! The last high reach of the spirit, matter's rejection, the abstract core of religion which is purity, wonder and love.

Onto this roof top Benjamin Murphy steps out. He is momentarily stunned and blinded by the brilliance around him. He takes off his bookkeeper's glasses and flings them away, likewise the book containing the August sales records. From his pocket he removes the little bag of Golden Bantam corn. He scatters the grains moderately at first, then with reckless abandon, finally splitting the bag wide open and throwing all the remaining corn high in the air. —If it is feasible, there should be a few pigeons.

All at once the Girl steps out behind him. She is all in white like a swan and her thin white scarf is blown out wing-like behind her. They stare at each other raptly for several moments and there is a faint, faint whispering of music.

GIRL [*shyly smiling*]: Hello, Rabbit.

BEN: Hello, Alice. How did you get up here?

GIRL: You told me last night about the stairs to the roof. You made me promise I'd feed the pigeons after you leave, so here I am with a nickel's worth of Golden Bantam corn. [*The Girl scatters a handful in the air.*]

BEN [*wonderingly and joyfully regarding her*]: I never suspected that you would have the nerve to follow me up here.

GIRL: Didn't I follow you to Wonderland last night?

BEN: Yeah, but that was relatively easy. This is a lot more difficult than that.

GIRL: It doesn't matter how difficult a place may be to arrive at—if the *man* is *there*, the woman will ultimately grace that place with her presence. No matter how high it is—no matter how low it is—no matter how precariously suspended in the middle! —It becomes Wonderland to the woman the very instant that she can stretch out her hands and with the tips of her fingers touch the tips of his!

BEN: What a little idealist you are. You almost make me think it might be worth my while.

GIRL [*scattering grain*]: Worth your while to do what?

BEN: To undertake your further emancipation.

GIRL: You're so modest. How do you know it needs to be undertaken?

BEN: We'll see.

GIRL: We'll see, we'll see, we'll see—so far it takes my breath! There's the park where we went walking last night!

BEN: There's the fox-cage—empty!

GIRL: There's the lake.

BEN: Where I met the swan and you met a man named Warren.

GIRL [*laughing*]: Yes, a *rabbit*-warren.

BEN: There's the carnival grounds. The lights are out but tonight they'll come back on and Beauty will dance for the Beast and the acrobat will swing from the highest trapeze!

GIRL: Oh, don't let's ever go down from this high place.

BEN [*smiling strangely*]: Maybe it won't be necessary to.

GIRL: How can we avoid it?

BEN: By going *up*.

GIRL: We can't go up any further. We're on the roof already.

BEN: The roof! What roof! The roof is only the jumping-off place to a man with my ambitions.

[*Sound: great laughter.*]

GIRL [*awed and frightened*]: What's that?

BEN [*awed but* not *frightened*]: That? I don't know. But I've heard that sound before.

[*A clap of thunder is heard and a cloud of smoke rises. Mr. E appears on the roof. He wears his beautiful sky-blue robe sprinkled with cosmic symbols and in his hand he holds an enormous sparkler. Daylight has faded all of a sudden and the first few stars are beginning to emerge among the towers of stone. Mr. E's beard flows purely and whitely in the freshening wind of a summer twilight. There is a faint and lovely*] *strain of music from the turning spheres. The Girl clings timidly to Ben's arm but Ben steps boldly forward.*]

BEN: Hello, Doc. How are yuh?

MR. E [*deeply and graciously*]: Hello, Murphy. How do you do, young lady?

GIRL [*clinging to Ben's arm*]: We're—we're fine, I think.

MR. E: Ben Murphy!

BEN: Yes, sir?

MR. E: Did I understand you to say that you are a man whose ambitions extend beyond the roof?

BEN: That's right, Doc.

MR. E: Very good, Murphy. You may be the man we're looking for.

BEN: For—what?

MR. E: Murphy, how would you like to undertake the colonization of a brand-new star?

[*Pause—faint music is heard.*]

GIRL [*frightened*]: Oh, Rabbit!

BEN [*intrepidly*]: Which one is it, Doc?

MR. E: Why, that one, way up there. [*He points with his sparkler.*]

[*Ben peers through his cupped hands.*]

BEN: Aw, that one, huh? Gosh, it sure is bright. It looks brand new.

MR. E: We just turned it out this morning. We call it World Number Two.

BEN: Completely furnished?

MR. E: Everything that a man requires to live on.

GIRL: And a *woman*?

MR. E: Young lady, I am talking to Mr. Murphy.

GIRL: Oh, but you're talking to me, Mr.—

MR. E: Mr. E is the name—Mr. E!

GIRL [*agitated*]: You see—see—*see*, Mr. E—we're indissoluble partners, he and I!

BEN: Since when?

GIRL: Yesterday—and always!

BEN: I've got a wife.

MR. E: You *did* have a wife, Mr. Murphy. You wife has left you.

BEN: I'm going to have a baby.

MR. E: Definitely, Mr. Murphy! You're destined to be the father of untold millions.

BEN: On that—new star?

MR. E: On that new star!

BEN: Oh, then, then, —I—can't be a *bachelor*, then!

GIRL: No! You see?

BEN: Shhh! —Mr. E is talking!

MR. E: We have been thinking of trying out something new. Something that has only been tried so far in the vegetable kingdom. Our reason for this experiment is the rather sorry mess that having two sexes has made of things down here on World Number One.

BEN: How's that, Doc?

MR. E: I suppose you've heard of monosexual reproduction?

BEN: Huh? —Yes—*vaguely*!

MR. E: One sex doing the whole thing all by itself!

BEN: You mean—*me*? —Have babies?

MR. E: A man with your ambitions—why not, Mr. Murphy?

GIRL [*alarmed*]: Ohhhhhhhhhhh!

BEN [*terrified*]: Noooooooooooo! No dice, Doc!

MR. E: What?

BEN: I don't like the idea. What do *you* think, Doc? Sex is pleasant, but is it necessary?

MR. E: Well, Murphy, it's up to you.

BEN: *Me* have *babies*? All by *myself*? That's out! Sister, you've bought your ticket, she's comin' up there with me! —Or I don't go!

GIRL [*dancing with joy*]: Hooray—!

BEN: Come on, sweetheart! [*He picks up the Girl.*] How do we get there, Doc?

MR. E [*moving his sparkler in a wide circle*]:
    Jack be nimble!
    Jack be quick!
    Jack jump over—
             Arithmetic!

[*There is a blinding flash. Thunder. Smoke clouds the stage. Great laughter. When the smoke clears away, Murphy and the Girl have disappeared. Mr. E stands alone on the rooftop and there is a faint whistling sound and a delicate far-away music of the spheres. Mr. E. looks up and his laughter dies slowly out. He raises an arm and slowly wipes off a tear on the edge of his starry sleeve.*]

MR. E [*to the audience*]: What a fool I am. What a sentimental old fool I am. At last I come to the inescapable conclusion that I made a dreadful mistake when I created the race of man on earth. I decided to correct it by blotting the whole thing out. Good! — But what happens? My heavenly spyglass happens to fall on a little clerk named Murphy. No hero out of books, no genius, mind you, but just an ordinary little white-collar worker in a wholesale shirt corporation, a man whose earning capacity has never exceeded eighteen-fifty per week. At first I am only a little amused by his antics. Then I chuckle. Then I laugh out loud. Then all at once I find myself—weeping a little. [*He blows his nose on a starry handkerchief.*] This funny little clown of a man named Murphy has suddenly turned into the tragic protagonist of a play called "Human Courage." Yes, the wonderful, pitiful, inextinguishable courage of the race of man—has played me for a sucker once again. In the middle of my laughter—I suddenly cry. What do I do? Rectify the mistake, as planned, by fire and everlasting damnation? No. Quite the contrary. Instead of exterminating the human race, I send it off to colonize a brand-new star in heaven. [*He gazes raptly upward. His long beard flows in the wind. Music of the spheres is heard.*] Ah, well, there's no fool like an old fool, as they say— And I, by God, am the *oldest* fool of them *all*! [*With gentle laughter he raises the sparkler and begins to describe a circle.*]

> Jack be nimble!
> Jack be quick!
> Jack jump over—

[*Gum and the four stockholders suddenly burst out on to the roof.*]

GUM: Murphy! Murphy! Ben Murphy!

Q [*catching sight of Mr. E*]: Hey, Grampa, have you seen Murphy?

MR. E [*angrily*]: *Arithmetic!*

[*Flash of light. Thunder. Mr. E disappears in smoke. Distant band music.) With an anxious outcry, Mr. Gum rushes back to the door.*]

GUM: P! D! Q! T! We're being followed!

Q: Who by?

GUM: Everybody! They're all on the stairs to the roof!

[*The band is heard very distantly.*]

Q: Lock that door!

P: Hold it shut!

[*They mass against the door to the roof.*]

GUM [*assuming authority in the crisis*]: Don't try that. The jig is up. It's too late now to try to obstruct their progress.

[*The band music comes up.*]

Q [*frightened*]: What'll we do?

GUM: Smile, you sons of bitches! Act delighted. Play like this is what you always wanted!

[*They all assume false smiles and line up in a welcoming atti- tude by the door as all the employees of Continental Branch of Consolidated Shirtmakers troop gaily out on the roof. They cast their ledgers, their papers and pencils away with joyful cries of freedom.*]

EMPLOYEES [*together*]: We want Murphy, we want Murphy!

[*Thunder.*]

MURPHY [*from a long way off*]: Hello—good-bye, everybody!

[*There are loud cheers. The band strikes up a stirring martial air. Heavenly days! Bells are ringing all over the whole cre- ation! Roman candles and pinwheels are filling the pale blue* dusk with the most outrageous drunken jubilation! What is it? The Millennium? —Possibly! Who knows?

Voices in the crowd repeat, "What is it? The Millennium?" "The Millennium" grows to a repeated murmur as the crowd looks upward to where Ben has disappeared. Perhaps a banner reading THE MILLENNIUM appears from that direction.]

THE CURTAIN FALLS

THE END

AFTERWORD

Writers usually speak deprecatingly of their "early works" for they like to feel that their talents have greatly expanded with maturity. It is certainly true that the continued exercise of a craft breeds competence in it, but in writing there are other things besides competence. There are certain organic values, such as intensity of feeling, freshness of perception, moral earnestness and conviction. These are virtues that may exist in beginning writers and unfortunately they may exist more in the beginning than in the later stages. When I look back at "Stairs to the Roof" which I wrote six years ago—it seems like sixty years ago—I see its faults very plainly, as plainly as you may see them, but still I do not feel apologetic about this play. Unskilled and awkward as I was at this initial period in my playwriting, I certainly had a moral earnestness which I cannot boast of today, and I think that moral earnestness is a good thing for any times but particularly for these times. I wish I still had the idealistic passion of Benjamin Murphy! You may smile as I do at the sometimes sophomoric aspect of his excitement but I hope you will respect, as I do, the purity of his feeling and the honest concern which he had in his heart for the basic problem of mankind which is to dignify our lives with a certain freedom.

TENNESSEE WILLIAMS

(from the Pasadena Playhouse program, 1947)

New Directions Paperbooks—A Partial Listing

For a complete listing request free catalog from
New Directions, 80 Eighth Avenue, New York 10011

†Bilingual

For a complete listing request free catalog from
New Directions, 80 Eighth Avenue, New York 10011

†Bilingual